Crochet Crush

LAINE

Crochet Crush

MOLLA MILLS

Hardie Grant

BOOKS

Co

tents

Crocheting Around the World

A wooden box, filled with coloured balls of yarn, with a sign reading "Please, take some!", was placed along a walkway. I was about to go on a journey, or more precisely, I was about to turn my life upside down – and the shelves in my studio in Kallio, Helsinki, were full of yarn I no longer needed. Soon I would be a traveller without a home, voluntarily lost.

By that point, I had had several different professions. I had been a seamstress, an interior designer, a shopkeeper in a fabric store. But I had grown restless. I wanted to change course and follow the path of crochet – my real passion. Handcrafts had been an important part of my life

for years, and not a day had gone by without me making a double crochet or two.

So I made careful plans, packed up my home and my workroom and gave all my yarn away. In November 2015, it was time: I changed my woollen socks to flip-flops and switched the cold tarmac of Kallio for the humid Kerala tropics. I arrived in Thiruvananthapuram, amid the scents and greenery of southern India.

I remember us landing at a small airport surrounded by jungle. From there, we went along the muddy roads, searching for a rickshaw, trying to give way to the cows walking by. Thiruvananthapuram is known as the modern pearl of Kerala, a tech hub with close to a million inhabitants and numerous skyscrapers. I apparently missed all this, keeping my eyes on the immediate world around me.

The month I spent in India broadened my mind, but it wasn't until after my journey that I realised how much it had really changed me. In India, I learned how colours, flavours and sounds affect emotions and ways of thinking, and how much more I can get out of each experience when I use my senses to their full. Stay open and curious – you might find what I found in India closer than you think.

Hustle and bustle

As I passed the bridge over the Hudson River, the biting wind blew through my crochet shawl. Being made of alpaca, the surface of the shawl repelled both the drizzle and my tears of joy – but even though I had wrapped it around myself like a blanket, I was still freezing. I was looking at the Manhattan skyline with foggy eyes, feeling like I had been thrown into a movie set. This was it, the second leg of my DIY journey. I had travelled from India to the Big Apple, to a country where the air isn't filled with the scent of Javadhu herbs but with that of fries.

The fast pace of New York City made me feel dizzy. My own natural pace was born of time spent in the fields in Kurikka in Southern Ostrobothnia and in the gentle hum of the suburb of Kallio: in New York I felt left behind on day one! Behind the facade of constant hurry, there was a chance for exciting adventures, however. I witnessed a Broadway-level musical performance in the Union Square subway tunnel, enjoyed art with Harrison Ford in MoMa, and found that rundown small gallery by the little alleyway, with all the hidden gems.

All the rush and haste is a problem of modern society. It starts in the morning, continues through the day, slows down at night but doesn't stop.

That busy New York way of life had its effect on me too: I was constantly running everywhere but just didn't know where to. We think we are busy because we are surrounded by so many unfinished projects and so much entertainment we just cannot miss. When you feel the sense of rush creep up, grab your crochet work and start making. Even a short crochet break relaxes you, and helps you to slow down.

It wasn't until I reached the town of Woodstock, in the Catskills, north of New York, that I felt the hustle and bustle of the big city lift. As I let all the colours of Woodstock sink in, with an old-time distorted guitar sound as my soundtrack, I was truly present in every moment. When your fingers are busy creating something new, your mind is at ease.

Nevertheless, without a visa you can't continue your mindfulness exercises for ever. From the United States, my journey meandered on and my crochet work-in-progress I carried in my cabin bag was an endless source of conversation in airports.

One time, a young officer at Madrid airport asked me to step aside after the metal detector went off. He dug out all my crochet hooks, and I was certain I was about to lose all twenty of them. I was amazed when he instead told me that my tools had brought back memories of his grandmother. She was a crocheter, a lacemaker, and her magical skills had left a permanent mark on this young man's memories.

Nonverbal communication

I have travelled in many countries with my eyes wide open and my sketchbook in my hands, collecting ideas and inspiration, getting to know the local artisans and traditions. Through centuries, unique cultures have been woven into fabrics, embroidered on to accessories and crocheted into rugs all around the world. In handcraft museums worldwide, you

EVEN A SHORT CROCHET BREAK RELAXES YOU, AND HELPS YOU TO SLOW DOWN.

will find exhibitions showing traditions combined with modern textile work. However, I think the best way to get to the roots of handcrafts is to get to know local makers.

In the Teotitlán del Valle handicraft village in Oaxaca, Mexico, my teacher, Juana, told me about the usage of natural pigments in the weavings of the Zapotec people. My hands turned blue and crimson by turns as Juana and I dyed thick wool using indigo and carmine.

I was crocheting by Lake Atitlán in southwestern Guatemala when a group of old Mayan women gathered around me. I didn't immediately have a common language with these women, whose main source of livelihood is handcrafts, but the language of making is a universal, nonverbal one – our hands told the same tales.

In Santiago, I had just placed my juices and marra-queta on to the cash register when a woman recognised me. Visibly touched, she started telling me how my work had inspired her. My Spanish skills weren't sufficient to understand everything she was saying, but her gestures got the message across. It was a beautiful moment, and it reminded me of why I keep doing what I do.

All the crochet patterns in this book were created while travelling. Forget the rush and let handcrafts fill your days: let the vibrant colours recharge your batteries and get inspired!

Happy crocheting,

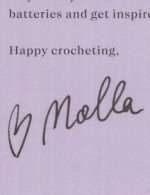

Keto blanket p. 140, Kerho duffel bag p. 52
Vuokko beach rug p. 208

Loiva mattress p. 114
Aita blanket p. 84

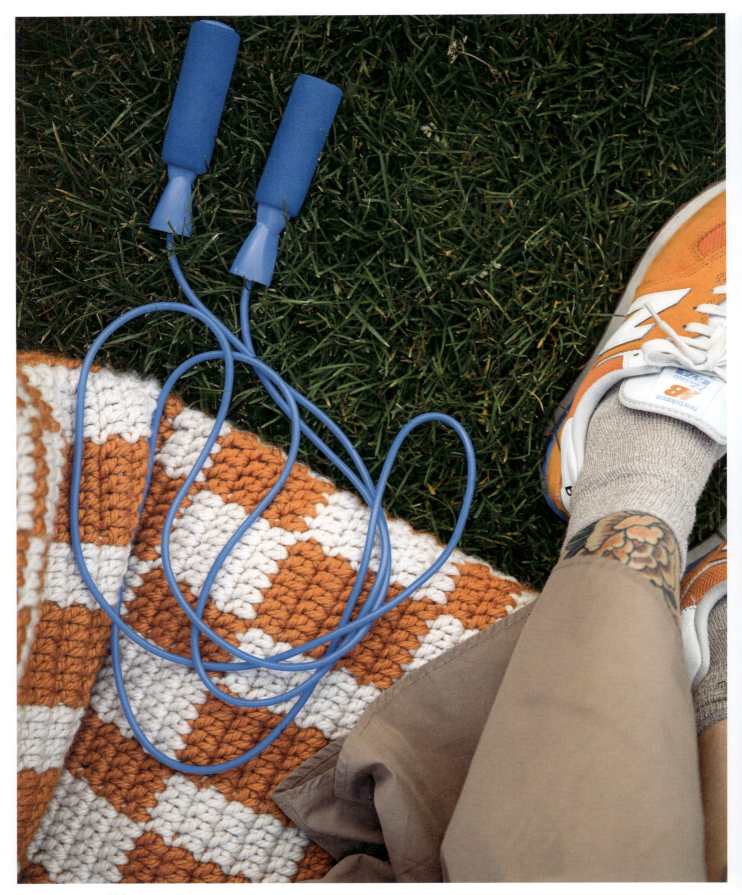

Ruutu mattress p. 164

Mansikka cushion p. 42

Tips for Crocheters

The greatest thing about crocheting is its simplicity. You begin with a loop of yarn that can grow from a single crochet stitch to a double crochet stitch or stay in between as a half double crochet stitch. Sometimes it can form a bobble-like popcorn stitch – or it can even be a mixture of all the above. Endless possibilities!

As crochet fabric has very little stretch, it is best used for home textiles and accessories such as bags and purses. You can crochet colourful patterns in a spiral or back and forth; work decreases and increases; shape the piece in multiple ways and join pieces together. Create something that best suits your needs.

In this section, I have put together some useful tips on tools, techniques and different stages of work.

Choosing yarn

Pick a natural material and go for your favourite colours or try something completely different instead. On each pattern page, you can find information about the yarn, how much of it you will need and the gauge. However, these are only suggestions and you are free to use other yarns instead. Try combining different materials – for example, alpaca and cotton make a beautiful combo. If you do this, make sure that your combination of yarns comes to the same thickness as the original yarn used in the pattern. If you want to match the pattern and its measurements as closely as possible, work a gauge swatch and compare that with the gauge given in the pattern.

Tools

A crochet work-in-progress is easy to carry with you everywhere as you only really need one tool: a crochet hook. They are usually made of plastic, wood or metal and you can even carve your own. Try out different crochet hooks from different manufacturers to find the one that works best for you. Pay attention to the handle of the hook – for example, a plastic handle on a metallic hook makes it more ergonomic and enjoyable to use. Other tools you will need to complete the projects in this book are scissors, a tape measure and a tapestry needle.

How to hold your hook

There might be a ton of different hooks to choose from, but there are only two ways of holding a crochet hook: the pencil hold and the knife hold. With the pencil hold, you have a lighter grip on the hook, so for crochet hooks that are 7 mm (K-10 ½) and larger, it is advisable to use the knife hold. This makes crocheting easier for your wrists and you can crochet something heavier for hours.

Getting started

A crochet work often begins with making a slip knot. From there, you'll continue to work a beginning or foundation chain, creating the number of chain stitches stated in the pattern. Always remember to leave a yarn tail long enough for weaving in. Another way of starting a crochet project is to loop the yarn around your finger and crochet into this loop. The squares in the Smile shoulder bag are worked in this manner.

When you are working in closed rounds, such as in the Loiva mattress, pay close attention to the number of stitches in the beginning chain. It is not possible to alter the number of stitches after you've closed the round. On the other hand, if you are working single crochet stitches back and forth, making the Aalto rug, for example, and you notice that you have too many stitches on your beginning chain, you can omit the extra stitches easily. Just open the slip knot and pull the extra stitches out. Also, if you are missing some stitches, you can always add a couple of stitches to the beginning of the foundation chain. This is where the long yarn tail will come in handy.

Pattern repeat

In many of the designs in this book, the pattern consists of *pattern repeats*. They are like building blocks that you can omit some of or work more of, depending on what size you wish the finished work to be. Pattern repeats are placed so that the pattern continues seamlessly throughout the work. The size of the pattern repeat is mentioned on the pattern page, so to make the work larger or smaller just omit or add a multiple of stitches mentioned for the pattern repeat.

Stitches

The most-used stitches in this book are the single crochet stitch, the double crochet stitch and the slip stitch.

The single crochet stitch can be worked back and forth or in a spiral, and also as a knit stitch, such as in the Vasu flower basket. Many of the rugs in the book are worked back and forth in single crochet stitches, which creates a surface where the stitches are vertically aligned. Worked in a spiral, single crochet stitches will form a diagonal pattern. *Knit stitches* can only be worked in a spiral, but the structure of the stitch will still create straight lines in the pattern. In addition, there is also the *optical crochet technique* that I showcased in my previous books. In this technique, you work the single crochet stitch in a spiral but pick up only the front yarn loop of a stitch. This will keep the pattern straight.

Double crochet stitches, on the other hand, will align on top of one another whether you are working both back and forth or in a spiral. A *slip stitch* is used for finishing and seaming – it can be used to reinforce the edges of a piece and also for joining pieces together.

Please note that every knitter has their own natural tension when crocheting, which will affect the outcome. A yarn over from the front side of the hook creates a different kind of surface to a yarn over from the back side of the hook. Being left or right-handed might also affect the finished piece.

The size of the piece depends on both the yarn you are using and the type of stitch used. Most of the rugs in the book are crocheted with a thick yarn, using single crochet stitches, but if you choose to use a thinner yarn, you can also change the type of stitch used. You can change a single crochet pattern into a double crochet pattern by crocheting two double crochet stitches for each single crochet stitch – this will also double the size of the piece.

You can also do the opposite and work two single crochet stitches for each double crochet stitch. The Loiva pillow, worked using the pattern for the Loiva mattress, is a good example of this substitution.

Tapestry crochet

You can create cheerfully colourful pieces by crocheting with multiple colours and carrying the other yarns inside the stitches. You can use up to five or six different colours. The colour changes follow the pattern and you can make the piece using either single or double crochet stitches. In tapestry crochet, you always change the colour of the yarn on the last yarn over of the stitch – remember to pay close attention to the tension of the yarns. Always work tapestry crochet with as small a hook as possible to make the surface dense enough so the carried yarns will not show on the right side of the work.

When you run out of yarn

When you run out of yarn in the middle of the work, tie the old and new yarn together and leave an approximately 10 cm (4 in) tail for weaving in. If you want, you can weave the tails into the stitches. If you're using a thick yarn, such as the Matilda yarn used for the Polku rug, crochet the new yarn together with the stitches for about 15 cm (6 in). Then change to the new yarn without tying the yarns together, and finally weave in about 15 cm (6 in) of the tails.

Finishing

Different kinds of crochet works require different methods of finishing. I often work a slip stitch row on both ends of rugs to make them more durable. It can also prevent the ends of the rug from curling inwards, but the best way to stop this from happening is to sew cotton tape on to the wrong side of the work. The edges of bags and baskets are also finished with a row of slip stitches. On projects that have been crocheted with double crochet stitches, I prefer to reinforce the edges with a row of single crochet stitches instead. For example, in the Smile bag, you work several rows of single crochet stitches to first create a border that is then folded in half.

You can also block the finished work to measurements and steam it lightly. Ironing is not recommended as the heat might flatten the stitches. The rugs do not need steaming or blocking, but if the edges of the rug seem wavy, get a friend and pull the rug tightly from opposite corners to make the stitches set in place.

Modifications

You can use the patterns featured in this book in multiple ways. You can modify the size of the pattern and change the colours or the materials. Pick a pattern that best suits the project you are planning – for example, with rugs you can go for a bigger, bolder pattern. Feel free to play around with which pattern to use for which project – you can use the design of a rug to crochet a bag: just choose a thinner cotton yarn instead of a thicker twine. Most of the designs in the book can be worked in a spiral or back and forth. You can make a pattern larger or smaller by choosing another crochet stitch to use. See more about this in the Stitches section.

Branding

Your finished crochet work should reflect its maker, so be bold and make it your own! Use a statement combination of colours or accessorize your piece with unique handles, fastenings, logos and lining materials. I have sewn my own round leather logo on to the works in this book, to give them that special designer look. For the handles, I have chosen undyed tanned leather. The metallic locks and other fastenings are chrome-coloured (I have collected them from my travels around the world). The most important sign of my brand, however, is that each piece is made locally and with my own hands.

Stitches and Abbreviations

rnd = round, rounds. When working back and forth, you work in rows. When working in a spiral, you work in rounds.

ch = chain stitch. Most crochet patterns begin by making a slip knot and then working chain stitches.

st = stitch (sts = stitches).

yoh = yarn over hook. Roll yarn over a hook from the backside of the hook.

sc = single crochet stitch (Am.). Put the hook through a stitch, take a yoh and pull to the right side of the work, take a yoh and pull through two loops on the hook.

kst = knit stitch. Put the hook through the middle of a stitch, take a yoh and pull to the right side of the work, take a yoh and pull through two loops on the hook. Knit stitch is a single crochet stitch, but more robust. You can work a knit stitch only in rounds.

sdc = starting double crochet stitch. Loosen up the loop on your hook, put your finger on top of the loop and keep it in place, circle the hook around the loop from the right side, take a yoh and pull through the first loop on your hook. Then put the hook through the starting stitch (slip stitch, if you are changing rounds), take a yoh, and pull to the right side of the work, take a yoh and pull through two loops, take a yoh and pull through two loops. This stitch is similar to the double crochet stitch.

dc = double crochet stitch (Am.). Take a yoh, put the hook through a stitch, take a yoh and pull to the right side of the work, take a yoh and pull through two loops, take a yoh and pull through two loops.

half-dc = half double crochet stitch. Take a yoh, put the hook through a stitch, take a yoh and pull to the right side of the work, take a yoh and pull through three loops.

long-dc = long double crochet stitch. Take two yoh, put the hook through a stitch, take a yoh and pull to the right side of the work, take a yoh and pull through two loops, take a yoh and pull through two loops, take a yoh and pull through two loops.

super-dc = super-long double crochet stitch. Take three yoh, put the hook through a stitch, take a yoh and pull to the right side of the work, take a yoh and pull through two loops, take a yoh and pull through two loops, take a yoh and pull through two loops, take a yoh and pull through two loops.

pop = popcorn stitch. Work 6 dc in the next st, remove hook from the loop, grab the top two loops of the first dc of pop on your hook, pull the yarn loop of the last dc of the pop through the st. Make sure your popcorn forms on the right side of the work.

bob = bobble stitch. Take a yoh, put the hook through the next stitch, take a yoh and pull a 1 cm (½ in) long yarn loop on the right side of the work, repeat the same altogether 6 times, then take a yoh and pull all the loops tightly together from the top. The yarn loops form a soft round bobble in the work.

sl st = slip stitch. Put the hook through a stitch, take a yoh and pull to the right side of the work, then pull the same loop through all loops on the hook. Slip stitch is used in closing the rounds and finishing the edges.

Work all loops on the two topmost yarn loops of a stitch (excluding the knit stitch).

When working in multiple colours, always change the colour of the yarn in the last yoh of the stitch.

Kontti

Moving house is one of the most stressful tasks – especially if you have cupboards and bookshelves filled with yarn. When I decided years ago to go explore the world, I found myself stuck with my fibre mountain. I could not possibly fit all those balls of yarn and twine into my storage unit.

Back then, I could maybe have crocheted these kinds of big boxes to store the rest of my yarns. On the other hand, I feel that crocheting, as with life in general, is about change and renewal, going with the flow and letting go.

Kontti box

SIZE	w. 26 cm, h. 14 cm, d. 20 cm (w. 10 ¼ in, h. 5 ½ in, d. 8 in)
YARN	Filona jute cord, Lankava (100% jute, 500 g roll = 225 m / 1 lb 2 oz roll = 246 yards, Tex 280 x 8), pink 600 g (1 lb 5 oz)
HOOK	5 mm (H-8)
GAUGE	6 sc x 6 rows = 5 x 5 cm (2 x 2 in)

INFO

The box is worked in rounds around the foundation chain in single crochet stitches. Add stitches in all four corners on each round to make the work grow seamlessly. Make a separate basket and a lid.

ABBREVIATIONS

rnd = round, rounds
ch = chain stitch
st = stitch
sc = single crochet
sl st = slip stitch

INSTRUCTIONS

BASE

Work 8 chain stitches to begin.

RND 1. Work 3 sc in the second st from the hook. Work 1 sc in the next 5 sts, 3 sc in the last st. Turn and work the sts on the other edge of the foundation chain. Work 1 sc in the next 5 sts, continue to the second round in a spiral.

RND 2. Work 3 sc in the first st, 1 sc, 3 sc in the next st. Work 1 sc in the next 5 sts, 3 sc in the next st, 1 sc, 3 sc in the next st, 1 sc in the next 5 sts.

RND 3. Work 1 sc, work 3 sc in the corner st, 1 sc in the next 3 sts, 3 sc in the corner st, 1 sc in the next 7 sts, 3 sc in the corner st, 1 sc in the next 3 sts, 3 sc in the corner st, 1 sc in the next 7 sts.

RNDS 4–12. Continue working with the same pattern, work 3 sc in all corners, 1 sc in other sts.

RND 13. Work 1 sc, work 1 sc in the corner st, work the next 2 sc together (decrease), work 1 sc in the next 19 sts, work the next 2 sc together, 1 sc in the corner st, 2 sc together, 1 sc in the next 23 sts, 2 sc together, 1 sc in the corner, 2 s together, 1 sc in the next 19 sts, 2 sc together,
1 sc in the corner, 2 sc together, 1 sc in the next 23 sts. At the end of the round, skip first sc and continue to a new round.

RNDS 14–25. Work 1 sc in each st.

Work a slip stitch round on the top edge of the work. Cut yarn and weave in ends.

LID

Work the lid as for the basket from round 1 to round 12.

RND 13. Work as round 12. The lid is one round bigger than the base.

RND 14. Work 1 sc, work 1 sc in the corner, work the next 2 sc together (decrease), work 1 sc in the next 21 sts, 2 sc together, 1 sc in the corner, 2 sc together. Work 1 sc in the next 25 sts, 2 sc together, 1 sc in the corner, 2 sc together, 1 sc in the next 21 sts, 2 sc together, 1 sc in the corner, 2 sc together, 1 sc in the next 25 sts. At the end of the round, skip the first sc and continue to a new round.

RNDS 15–17. Work 1 sc in each st.

Work a slip stitch round on the top edge of the work. Cut yarn and weave in ends.

Kontti

Chart, base

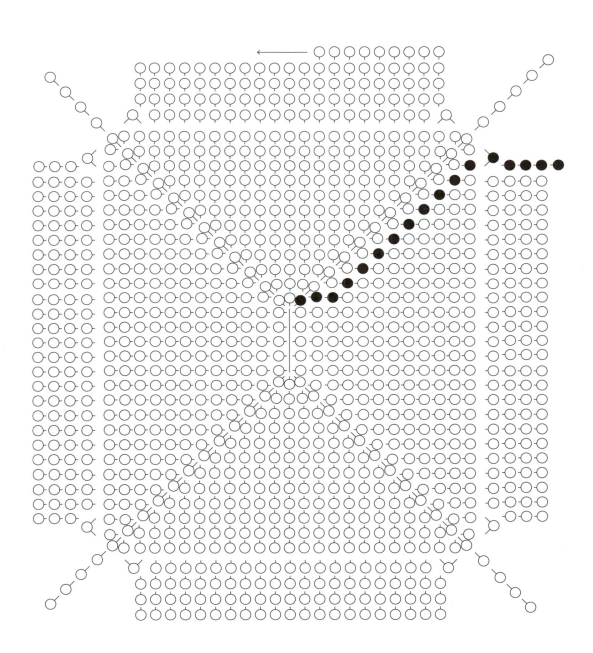

foundation chain	● first st of the round
○ single crochet stitch, sc	⨂ decrease, 2 sc worked together

corner increase, 3 sc worked in a same st

Mansikka

My mother has been growing strawberries in her garden for as long as I can remember. She would always make strawberry juice and jam with all the berries that were left behind after we kids, along with the birds and cats, had gotten our share. Me and my siblings would also pick wild strawberries from the meadows nearby. I have grown so fond of that familiar taste of Finnish strawberries, that when I am abroad I don't dare to buy the local strawberries but go for other fruits instead.

Strawberry plants have beautiful flowers with white petals and I have also crocheted those on to the Mansikka pocket. I wonder what this design would look like with those beautifully ripe berries?

Mansikka pocket

SIZE	w. 15 cm, h.18 cm (w. 6 in, h. 7 in)
YARN	leftover yarns, beige cotton 100 g (3 ½ oz), white and yellow wool 50 g (1 ¾ oz) per colour
HOOK	1.75 mm (US steel 6 / 7)
GAUGE	18 dc x 8 rnds = 5 x 5 cm (2 x 2 in)
OTHER	thin leather strap 70 cm (27 ½ in), two snap hooks

INFO

The pocket is worked in closed rounds in double crochet, popcorn, and bobble stitches, carrying the other yarns inside the stitches throughout the work. Make sure not to pull the carry-on yarn too tight, keep it loose. Change the colour of the yarn in the last yarn over of the stitch.

ABBREVIATIONS

rnd = round, rounds
ch = chain stitch
st = stitch
sdc = starting double crochet stitch
sc = single crochet
dc = double crochet
pop = popcorn stitch
bob = bobble stitch
yoh = yarn over hook
sl st = slip stitch

INSTRUCTIONS

Work 47 chain stitches in beige yarn to begin.

RND 1. Work 2 dc in the fourth st from the hook. Grab the other yarns in the work. Work 1 dc in the next 42 sts. Work 6 dc in the last st, turn and continue working on the other edge of the foundation chain. Work 1 dc in the next 42 sts. Work 3 dc in the starting st, close round with a sl st. You have 96 dc in the work.

RND 2. Work a sdc, grab the other yarns in the work. Work 1 dc in each st, close with a sl st.

RND 3. Work a sdc, grab the other yarns in the work. Work 4 p, change to white yarn in the last yoh. Work a popcorn stitch, pop; work 6 dc in the next st (change to beige yarn in the last yoh), remove hook from the loop, grab the top two loops of the first dc of pop on your hook, pull the yarn loop of the last dc of the pop through the st. *Hey! Make sure your popcorn forms on the right side of the work. Push the stitches gently with a finger.* Work 1 dc in beige yarn, 1 pop in white yarn. Work *9 dc in beige yarn, 1 pop in white yarn 1 dc in black yarn, 1 pop in white yarn*, repeat *–* altogether 8 times. Work 4 dc in beige yarn, close round with a sl st.

You have 96 dc in the work, which is 8 pattern repeats. The size of one pattern repeat is 12 dc in width and 8 rounds in height.

RND 4. Work a sdc, grab the other yarns in the work. Work 3 dc, change to white yarn in the last yoh. Work 1 pop, change to yellow yarn in the last yoh, work 1 dc. Work a bobble stitch, bob; *pull a yoh, put the hook through the next st, pull a 1 cm (½ in) long yarn loop*, repeat *–* altogether 6 times, then take a yoh and pull all the loops together. Work 1 dc, change to white yarn in the last yoh, work 1 pop. Change to black yarn, work 7 dc. Work *1 pop in white yarn, change to yellow yarn, work 1 dc, 1 bob, 1 dc, change to white yarn, work 1 pop, change to beige yarn, work 7 dc*, repeat *–* altogether 8 times. Work 3 dc in beige yarn, close round with a sl st.

RND 5. Work a sdc, grab the other yarns in the work. Work 4 dc in beige yarn, 2 dc in the next st, change to white yarn in the last yoh. Work a half-pop; work 3 in the next st, 3 dc in the following st, remove hook from the loop, grab the top two loops of the first dc of pop on your hook, pull the yarn loop of the last dc of the pop through the st. Work 9 dc in beige yarn. Work *2 dc in the next st with beige yarn, 1 half-pop in the next 2 sts in white yarn, 9 dc in beige yarn*, repeat *–* altogether 8 times. Work 4 dc in beige yarn, close round with a sl st.

RNDS 6–26. Work altogether 26 rounds (3 vertical pattern repeats), with the first 2 rounds and the last round worked in beige yarn.

RND 27. Cut white and yellow yarn and weave in ends. Continue with beige yarn. Work 2 slip sts and work the lid.

○	chain, ch
ᛦ	starting double crochet stitch, sdc
⊤⊤	double crochet stitch, dc
Ϲ Ϲ Ϲ	slip stitch, sl st
⊕	popcorn stitch, pop, 6 dc worked together
◉	bobble stitch, bob, 6 yarn over sts worked together
ᚢ	increase, 2 dc worked in a same st
⊕	pop increase, 3 dc and 3 dc worked together
♀	single crochet stitch, sc

Mansikka

Chart

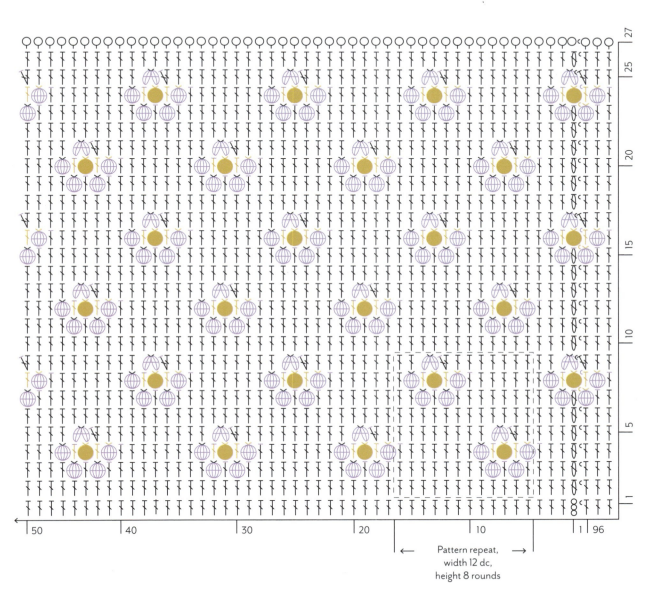

Pattern repeat,
width 12 dc,
height 8 rounds

Base of the work

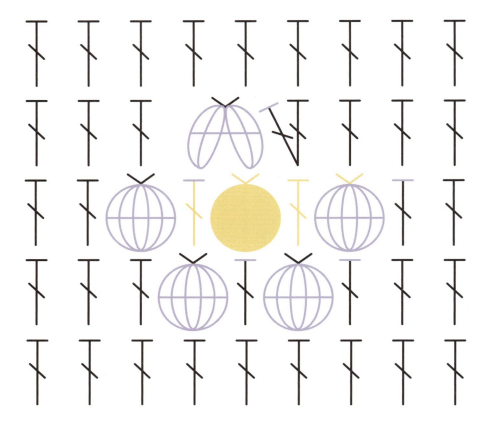

Mansikka pattern, detail from a chart.

LID

Work 2 ch, work 43 dc in beige yarn. Turn, work 2 ch, work
1 dc in each st. Continue working the lid with the same
pattern, work altogether 12 rows. Work a sc row on the
top edge, cut yarn and weave in ends.
Attach the snap hooks into the leather handle and put the
handle in place.

MANSIKKA CUSHION is worked according to the Mansikka pocket pattern. The circumference of the work is 96 dc and the height is 21 rounds.

After finishing the crochet piece, place the inner cushion inside the work and close the top seam with sc sts. Attach the leather handle in the middle of the top seam.

SIZE w. 50 cm, h. 50 cm (w. 19 ¾ in, h. 19 ¾ in)
YARN Lankava Muhku wool (100% wool, 1 kg roll = 390 m / 2 lb 3 oz roll = 426 yd, Tex 850 x 3), light brown 1 kg (2 lb 3 oz), natural white 600 g (1 lb 5 oz), orange 200 g (7 oz)
HOOK 7 mm (K-10 ½/L-11)
GAUGE 10 dc x 5 rnds = 10 x 10 cm (4 x 4 in)
OTHER leather handle, inner cushion 50 x 50 cm (19 ¾ x 19 ¾ in)

Kerho

Every journey begins by choosing the right bag to take with you. The day I waited for my flight to Delhi, India, was freezing. I was wearing the knee-high woollen socks my friend had knitted me, but in the end what kept me warm was the huge rucksack I was carrying on my back. I had packed lightly, trying to choose only the bare essentials, so it was not what was in the rucksack that kept me warm rather than what it represented: my excitement, openness and enthusiasm.

If you are longing for a change, you do not need to travel as far as India – just a couple of days outside of your everyday life gives so much new energy. The Kerho duffel bag is the perfect choice for a trip like this. You can carry it either over your shoulder or on your back.

Kerho duffel bag

SIZE	w. 40 cm, d. 25 cm (w. 15 ¾ in, d. 10 in)
YARN	Mini tube yarn by Lankava (80% recycled cotton, 20% polyester, 1 kg roll = 335 m / 2 lb 3 oz roll = 366 yd), orange 1 kg (2 lb 3 oz). Molla twine, 12-ply, by Suomen Lanka (100% cotton, 500 g roll = 1280 m / 1 lb 2 oz roll = 1400 yd, Tex 30 x 12), brown 150 g (5 ½ oz). A small amount of 12-ply natural white Liina twine for a name tag.
HOOK	5 mm (H-8) and 2 mm (US steel 4) for the name tag
GAUGE	13 sc x 13 rows = 10 x 10 cm (4 x 4 in)
OTHER	Openable zipper 45 cm (17 ¾ in), cotton ribbon 1 m (39 in), strong cotton strap 2.20 m (87 in) and 1.10m (43 in) for the shoulder strap, two snap hooks, two openable metal D-rings 45 mm (1 ¾ in), a buckle

INFO

The bag is worked back and forth in single crochet stitches with two yarns simultaneously. Work a big bag piece and two round side pieces, the side pieces are worked in rounds in single crochet stitches. Join the pieces together with a slip stitch seam.

ABBREVIATIONS

rnd = round, rounds
ch = chain stitch
st = stitch
sc = single crochet stitch
sl st = slip stitch

INSTRUCTIONS

BAG PIECE, RECTANGLE

Work 51 chain stitches to begin, leave a 4 m long yarn tail for the slip stitch row.

ROW 1. Work 1 sc in the second st from the hook. Work 1 sc in each st, you have 50 sc in the row.

ROWS 2–102. Work 1 ch, as this is the first sc of each row, work 1 sc in each st.

Work a slip stitch row on both ends of the work. Cut yarns and weave in ends.

SIDE PIECE, ROUND

RND 1. Roll yarn around a finger, work 8 sc in it. Work along the yarn tail, at the end of the round pull the yarn tail tight to close the hole. Jump to a new round in a spiral without a visible seam.

RND 2. Work 2 sc in each st (16 sc).

RND 3. Work 2 sc in every second st, work 1 sc in other sts (24 sc).

RND 4. Work 2 sc in every third st, work 1 sc in other sts (32 sc).

RND 5. Work 2 sc in every fourth, work 1 sc in other sts (40 sc).

RND 6. Work 2 sc in every fifth st, work 1 sc in other sts (48 sc).

RND 7. Work 2 sc in every sixth st, work 1 sc in other sts (56 sc).

RND 8. Work 2 sc in every seventh st, work 1 sc in other sts (64 sc).

RND 9. Work 2 sc in every eighth st, work 1 sc in other sts (72 sc).

RND 10. Work 2 sc in every ninth st, work 1 sc in other sts (80 sc).

RND 11. Work 2 sc in every tenth st, work 1 sc in other sts (88 sc).

RND 12. Work 2 sc in every 11th st, work 1 sc in other sts (96 sc).

RND 13. Work 2 sc in every 16th st, work 1 sc in other sts (102 sc).

RND 14. Work 1 sc in each st.

Leave a 4 m (157 in) long yarn tail for the slip stitch row. Cut yarn. Work another similar piece..

NAME TAG

Work 48 chain stitches to begin, close ring with a slip stitch.

RND 1. Work 1 ch, work 1 sc in each st. Close round with a sl st.

RND 2. Work 3 ch and 2 dc in the same st, 1 dc, 6 sc, 1 dc, 5 dc in the next st, 1 dc, 12 sc, 1 dc, 5 dc in the next st, 1 dc, 6 sc, 1 dc, 5 dc in the same st, 1 sc, 12 sc, 1 dc, and 2 dc in the starting st. Close round with a sl st.

RND 3. Work 1 ch, work 1 sc in the same st, work 1 sc in the next 18 sts, 3 sc in the corner st, 1 sc in the next 12 sts, 3 sc in the corner st, 1 sc in the next 18 sts, 3 sc in the corner st, 1 sc in the next 12 sts, 1 sc in the first st. Close round with a sl st. Leave a 1.5 m long yarn tail for sewing. Cut yarn.

SEWING

Sew the openable zipper on the top edge of the bag inside the work, leave the zipper 3 cm from both ends. Sew a cotton ribbon to cover the zipper seam allowance by hand.

Place the work on a table right side up, mark the place for the long handle (2.2 m). The handle is sewn by hand 10 cm from both sides and 13 rows from both ends starting from the bottom of the bag. The length of the handle is 50 cm on both ends. (See the measurements on the following page).

Place the name tag on the right side of the bag, 17 rows from the top. Sew the name tag in place by hand.

Next, join the bag piece and the other side piece together with a slip stitch seam. Place the side piece and the bag piece together right sides out, start working from the bottom. Work a full round, cut yarn and weave in ends. Join the other side piece with the same pattern.

Attach one snap hook in the shorter handle (1.10 m), then weave in the buckle, attach the other snap hook. Next, attach the openable metal rings on top of the bag on both ends, and put the shoulder strap in place.

Kerho

Chart, name tag

◯	chain, ch
● ●	first st of the round
♀	single crochet stitch, sc
⊤	double crochet stitch, dc
(	slip stitch, sl st

Measurement chart

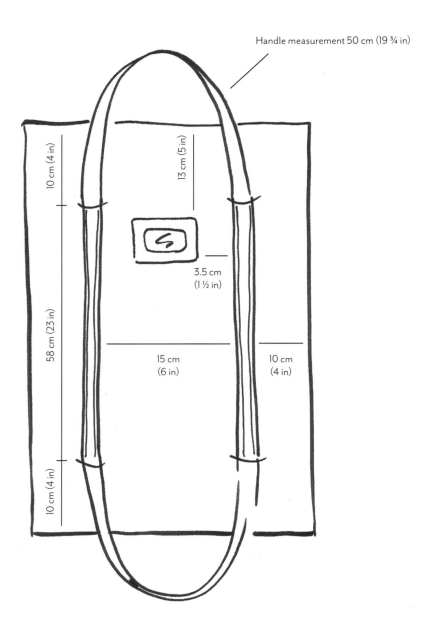

Handle measurement 50 cm (19 ¾ in)

13 cm (5 in)

10 cm (4 in)

58 cm (23 in)

10 cm (4 in)

3.5 cm (1 ½ in)

15 cm (6 in)

10 cm (4 in)

A long handle (2.2 m) is placed on top of the crochet bag piece according to the measurements. Sew handle in place with a strong thread.

Sol

Everything looks better seen through an orange sun visor. The bright colour radiates warmth and the shade will protect your eyes from damaging sun rays, but most importantly the visor – with a strap that looks like a sweatband – will make you cool. The text on the strap, "Here comes the sun," is borrowed from the Beatles, one of the greatest bands of all time. Through their lyrics they brought the sun to even the gloomiest rainy day in London.

You don't need to save this visor only for sunny days: being made with twine, it can take all weathers, concerts and gigs.

Sol visor

SIZE	w. 4 cm, l. 65 cm (w. 1 ½ in, l. 25 ½ in)
YARN	Liina twine, 12-ply, by Suomen Lanka (100% cotton, 500 g roll = 1280 m / 1 lb 2 oz roll = 1400 yd, Tex 30 x 12), black 50 g (1 ¾ oz), natural white 50 g (1 ¾ oz)
HOOK	1.75 mm (US steel 6 / 7)
OTHER	plastic visor, velcro 5 cm (2 in), 3 cm (1 ¼ in) wide cotton ribbon 40 cm (15 ¾ in)

INFO

The strap of the sun visor is worked back and forth in single crochet stitches, carrying the other yarn inside the stitches throughout the work. Make sure not to pull the carry-on yarn too tight, keep it loose. Leave the carry-on yarn one stitch from the end of each row to make sure the yarn loops will not show on the right side of the work. Change the colour of the yarn in the last yarn over of the stitch.

ABBREVIATIONS

ch = chain stitch
st = stitch
sc = single crochet stitch
yoh = yarn over hook
sl st = slip stitch

INSTRUCTIONS

Work 13 chain stitches in natural white yarn to begin.

ROW 1. Work 1 sc in the second st from the hook, grab the black yarn in the work. Work 1 sc in each st, you have 12 sc in the row. Leave the black yarn one st from the end at the backside of the work.

ROWS 2–30. Work 1 ch, grab the black yarn in the work, work 1 sc in each st.

ROW 31. Work 1 ch, 1 sc in natural white yarn, change to black yarn in the last yoh, work 8 sc, change to natural white yarn, work 2 sc.

ROWS 32–166. Follow the pattern chart.

Work 30 more rows with natural white yarn, carry the black yarn inside the sts throughout the work. Cut yarns and weave in ends.

SEWING

Place the plastic visor in the middle of the crochet piece at the lower edge of the work, at backside of the work. Sew the visor into the crochet piece by hand using strong sewing yarn, make sure the stitches are not showing on the right side of the work.

Sew the cotton ribbon at the backside of the crochet piece by hand, make sure the ribbon covers the seam allowance of the visor. The non-elastic cotton ribbon is shorter than the crochet piece, this allows the crochet piece to stretch a bit.

Measure place for the velcro fastening, sew the velcro pieces at both ends of the crochet piece according to your own measurements.

Sol Chart

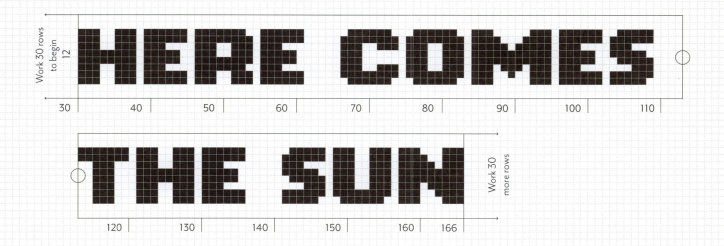

Work 30 rows to begin
12

30   40   50   60   70   80   90   100   110

120   130   140   150   160   166

Work 30 more rows

Single crochet stitch, sc

Kaunokki

The Kaunokki rug is colour therapy at its best – its sun-kissed tones bring a beautiful atmosphere to your home. Colours have a huge effect on our sense of space, energy levels and mood. Colours draw our attention first when we walk into a space, so if you have something bold and colourful in your home, people tend to gather around it without even realising.

In the Kaunokki rug, I have combined two bright colours, pink and orange. You can instantly feel their energising effect when crocheting. I recommend choosing a bright colour combo, though the pattern works beautifully in black and white as well. By modifying the pattern, you can crochet a poster as well as the rug.

Kaunokki rug

SIZE	w. 130 cm, l. 220 cm (w. 51 in, l. 87 in)
YARN	Frotee loopy craft yarn by Lankava (80% recycled yarn, 20% polyester, 1.2 kg roll = 280 m / 2 lb 10 oz roll = 306 yd), orange 4 rolls, pink 4 rolls
HOOK	9 mm (M/N-13)
GAUGE	7 sc x 7 rows = 10 x 10 cm (4 x 4 in)

INFO

The rug is worked back and forth in single crochet stitches, carrying the other yarn inside the stitches throughout the work. Make sure not to pull the carry-on yarn too tight, keep it loose. Leave the carry-on yarn one stitch from the end of each row to make sure the yarn loops will not show on the right side of the work. Change the colour of the yarn in the last yarn over of the stitch.

ABBREVIATIONS

ch = chain stitch
st = stitch
sc = single crochet
yoh = yarn over hook
sl st = slip stitch

INSTRUCTIONS

Work 95 chain stitches in orange yarn to begin, leave an 8 m (8 ¾ yd) long yarn tail for the slip stitch row.

ROW 1. Work 1 sc in the second st from the hook, grab the pink yarn in the work. Work 15 sc in orange yarn, change to pink yarn in the last yoh. Work 2 sc in pink yarn, 28 sc in orange yarn, 2 sc in pink yarn, 28 sc in orange yarn, 2 sc in pink yarn, 16 sc in orange yarn. Leave the pink yarn one st from the end at the backside of the work.

You have 94 sc in the row, which is 3 pattern repeats and 2 sc sts on both sides. One pattern repeat is 30 sc in width and 34 rows in height.

ROWS 2–4. Work 1 ch in orange yarn, as this is the first sc of each row. Grab the pink yarn in the work and work as for row 1.

ROW 5. Work 1 ch in orange yarn, grab the pink yarn in the work. Work 4 sc, change to pink yarn. *Work 5 s in pink yarn, 6 sc in orange yarn, 2 sc in pink yarn, 6 sc in orange yarn, 5 sc in pink yarn, 6 sc in orange yarn*, repeat *–* until the end of the row. At the end of the row, work 5 sc in orange yarn instead of 6 sc.

ROW 6. Work as for row 5.

ROWS 7–142. Work altogether 142 rows according to the pattern (4 vertical pattern repeats, 2 rows on the bottom and 4 rows on the top).

Work a slip stitch row on both ends of the work in orange yarn. Cut yarns and weave in ends.

Kaunokki

Chart

Single crochet stitch, sc

Pattern repeat w. 30 sc, h. 34 rows

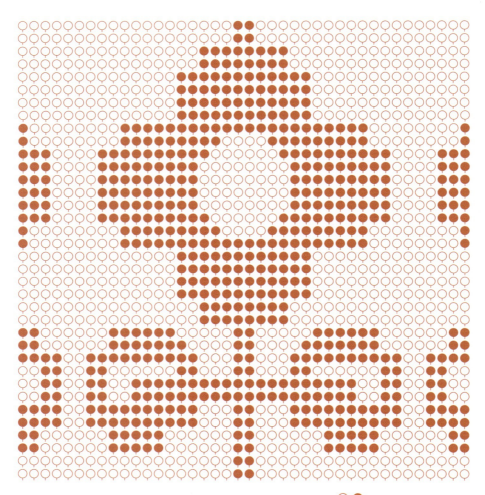

Kaunokki pattern, detail from a chart.  Single crochet stitch, sc

Kaunokki pattern can also be used to make an elegant pouch. This small and lightweight pouch is made in Liina Kalalanka 6-ply using natural white and black colours. Sew a zipper on the top opening and attach a handle, and the pouch is ready.

KAUNOKKI-POSTER Work the poster with a modified rug pattern. The poster is worked back and forth in double crochet stitches unlike the rug, which is worked in single crochet stitches. To change a single crochet pattern to a double crochet pattern simply work 2 double crochet stitches for every single crochet stitch.

The size of the poster is 188 dc in width and 108 rows in height.

SIZE w. 75 cm, h. 95 cm (w. 29 ½ in, h. 37 ½ in)
YARN Liina twine, 18-ply, by Suomen Lanka (100% cotton, 500 g roll = 840 m / 1 lb 2 oz roll = 875 yd, Tex 30 x 18), black 300 g (10 ½ oz), natural white 600 g (1 lb 5 oz)
HOOK 2.25 mm (B-1)
GAUGE 13 dc x 6 rows = 5 x 5 cm (2 x 2 in)

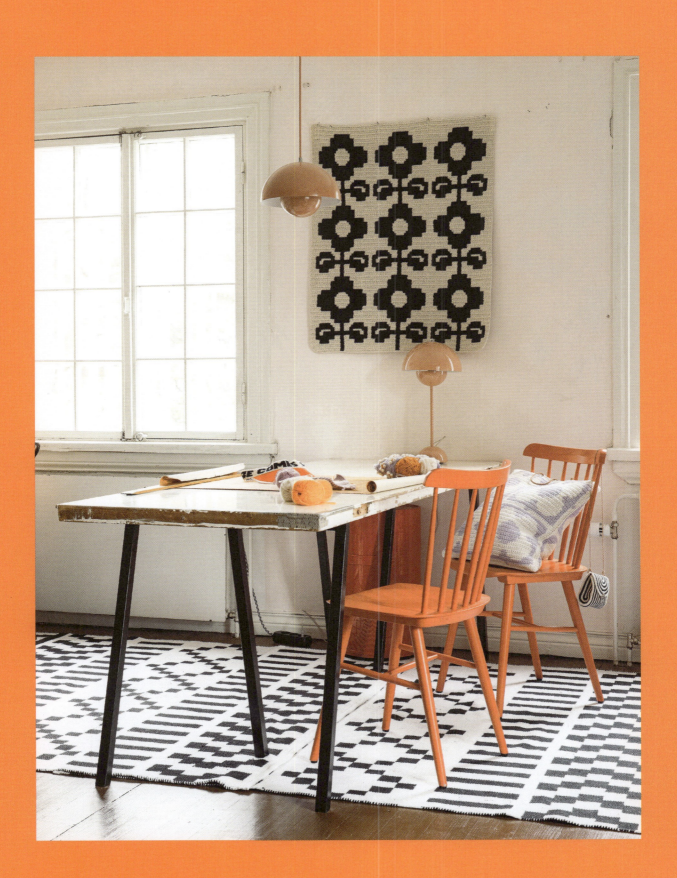

Leinikki

There are two things you can never have too many of: flowers and cushions. When I was living in Germany, I always had a bouquet of fresh flowers on a table. For only five euros I could get a colour burst for my gloomy apartment, tucked away in an inner courtyard. The lovely scents and colours invigorated my senses every morning and there was something magically soothing about those fresh flowers.

Cushions, on the other hand, are like giant building blocks in your living room. There are days when I feel like hiding from the daily rush inside a fortress of cushions. I would only leave a small opening in one of the walls: for me to get more yarn when I ran out.

In this book, the Leinikki cushion has been worked using black and white, but you should definitely test how the pattern would look crocheted with the bright yellow of a meadow buttercup.

Leinikki cushion

SIZE	d. 40 cm (15 ¾ in)
YARN	Varppi twine by Suomen Lanka (100% cotton, 500 g roll = 500 m / 1 lb 2 oz = 547 yd, Tex 50 x 18), black 300 g (10 ½ oz), natural white 100 g (3 ½ oz)
HOOK	3.5 mm (E-4)
GAUGE	8 dc x 4 rnds = 5 x 5 cm (2 x 2 in)
OTHER	round inner cushion d. 40 cm (15 ¾ in)

INFO

Work two hexagonal pieces for the cushion in rounds.
In the front piece, carry the other yarn in the work from
round 4 onwards. The back piece is worked solely in black
yarn. Join the pieces together with a single crochet stitch
seam.

ABBREVIATIONS

rnd = round, rounds

ch = chain stitch

st = stitch

sdc = starting double crochet stitch

dc = double crochet stitch

sc = single crochet stitch

yoh = yarn over hook

sl st = slip stitch

INSTRUCTIONS

FRONT PIECE

Cut a 1.5 m (59 in) long piece of black yarn for embroidery. Work the first 3 rounds solely in natural white yarn.

RND 1. Make a small yarn loop around a finger, close it with a sc, work 2 ch. Work 17 dc around the loop, carry the yarn tail in the work. Close round with a slip stitch. You have 18 dc in the work including the 2 ch. Pull the yarn tail to close the hole in the yarn loop.

RND 2. Work a sdc, work *2 dc in the next st, 2 dc in the next st, 1 dc*, repeat *–* until the end of the round (30 dc). Close all rounds with a slip stitch.

RND 3. Six small leaflets. Work a sdc, work *2 dc in the next st, 1 sc in the next 2 sts, 2 dc in the next st, 1 dc*, repeat *–* until the end of the round. Change to black yarn in the last yoh. Close with a sl st in the back loop of the st.

RND 4. Work 1 ch with black yarn, grab the natural white yarn in the work. Work *1 sc in the next 2 sts in the backside of the dc leaving the two topmost yarn loops on the front side of the work, work 2 dc in the next 2 sts taking both top loops of the st on your hook, 1 sc in the next 3 sts in the backside of the dc leaving the two topmost yarn loops at the front side of the work*, repeat *–* until the end of the round.

RND 5. Work a sdc with black yarn, grab the natural white yarn in the work. Work *1 dc in the next 3 sts, 2 dc in the next st, 1 ch, 2 dc in the next st, 1 dc in the next 4 sts*, repeat *–* until the end of the round. The width of one black petal is 11 dc.

RND 6. Work a sdc with black yarn, grab the natural white yarn in the work. Work *1 dc in the next 5 sts, 1 dc + 1 ch + 1 dc in the ch from the previous round, 1 dc in the next 6 sts*, repeat *–* until the end of the round. The width of one black petal is 13 dc.

RND 7. Work a sdc with black yarn, grab the natural white yarn in the work. Work *1 dc in the next 6 sts, change to natural white yarn in the last yoh, work 1 dc + 1 ch + 1 dc in the ch from the previous round in natural white yarn, change to black yarn, work 1 dc in the next 7 sts*, repeat *–* until the end of the round. The width of one black petal is 13 dc.

RND 8. Work a sdc with black yarn, grab the natural white yarn in the work. Work *1 dc in the next 6 sts, change to natural white yarn in the last yoh, work 1 dc, 1 dc + 1 ch + 1 dc in the ch, 1 dc in natural white yarn, change to black yarn, work 1 dc in the next 7 sts*, repeat *–* until the end of the round. The width of one black petal is 13 dc.

RND 9. Work a sdc with black yarn, grab the natural white yarn in the work. Work *1 dc in the next 5 sts, change to natural white yarn in the last yoh, work 1 dc in the next 3 sts, 1 dc + 1 ch + 1 dc in the ch, 1 dc in the next 3 sts in natural white yarn, change to black yarn, work 1 dc in the next 6 sts*, repeat *–* until the end of the round. The width of one black petal is 11 dc.

RND 10. Work a sdc with black yarn, grab the natural white yarn in the work. Work *1 dc in the next 3 sts, change to natural white yarn in the last yoh, work 1 dc in the next 6 sts, 1 dc + 1 ch + 1 dc in the ch, 1 dc in the next 6 sts in natural white yarn, change to black yarn, work 1 dc in the next 4 sts*, repeat *–* until the end of the round. Change to natural white yarn in the last yoh. The width of one black petal is 7 dc.

RND 11. Work a sdc with natural white yarn, grab the black yarn in the work. Work *1 dc in the next 10 sts, change to black yarn in the last yoh, work 1 dc + 1 ch + 1 dc in the ch with black yarn, change to natural white yarn, work 1 dc in the next 11 sts*, repeat *–* until the end of the round.

RND 12. Work a sdc with natural white yarn, grab the black yarn in the work. Work *1 dc in the next 9 sts, change to black yarn in the last yoh, work 1 dc in the next 2 sts, 1 dc + 1 ch + 1 dc in the ch, 1 dc in the next 3 sts in black yarn, change to natural white yarn, work 1 dc in the next 10 sts*, repeat *–* until the end of the round. Change to black yarn and work the last two rounds in black yarn only. Cut natural white yarn and weave in ends.

RND 13. Work a sdc, work 1 dc in each st, work 1 dc + 1 ch + 1 dc in each ch.

RND 14. Work a sdc, work 1 dc in each st, work 1 dc in each ch. You now have 168 dc in the work.

BACK PIECE

RND 1. Make a small yarn loop around a finger with black yarn, close it with a sc, work 2 ch. Work 17 dc around the loop, carry the yarn tail in the work. Close round with a slip stitch. You have 18 dc in the work counting in the 2 ch. Pull the yarn tail to close the hole in the yarn loop.

RND 2. Work a sdc, work *2 dc in the next st, 2 dc in the next st, 1 dc*, repeat *–* until the end of the round (30 dc). Close all rounds with a slip stitch.

RND 3. Work a sdc, work *1 dc, 2 dc in the next st, 1 ch, 2 dc in the next st, 1 dc in the next 2 sts*, repeat *–* until the end of the round.

RNDS 4–13. Work a sdc, work *1 dc in each st, work 1 dc + 1 ch + 1 dc in each ch from the last round*, repeat *–* until the end of the round. The work grows in each round.

RND 14. Work a sdc, work 1 dc in each st, work 1 dc in each ch from the previous round. Close round with a sl st (168 dc). Cut yarn and weave in ends.

FINISHING

Embroider the black round shape in the front piece between rounds 2 and 3.

Place the front piece and the back piece together right sides out, make sure all six corners meet. Crochet the pieces together with a seam of single crochet stitches. Before finishing the seam, place the inner cushion inside the work, and now finish the seam. Cut yarn and weave in ends.

Leinikki Chart

Front piece

◯ starting loop	ꓦ	increase, 2 dc worked in a same st
ο ○ chain, ch	((	slip stitch, sl st
ꝑ Ꝓ starting double crochet stitch, sdc	ọ ọ	single crochet stitch, sc
ꓕ double crochet stitch, dc	ọ	sc worked in a back loop of a st

Back piece

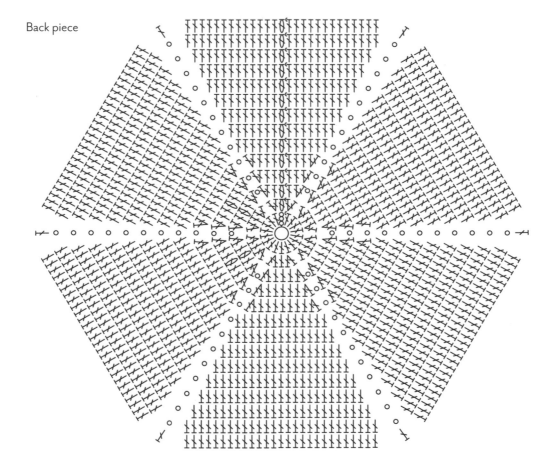

Aita

The traffic sign at Red Hook in Brooklyn read "Dead End". I was looking at the two words using the flashlight on my mobile phone. The night had fallen and I had no idea how I would get back to my pad at Crown Heights – clearly it was not the street on the left, as I had thought. It had been easy to get out of Manhattan, as the streets follow a similar pattern to this blanket – they form a simple grid. The edges of the blanket are more like Brooklyn. The twisting and sprawling mix of streets is here mimicked by a similar border of chain stitches.

Crocheted with a woollen yarn, the Aita blanket will keep you warm on a picnic and afterwards you can wrap it around yourself on the bicycle ride home.

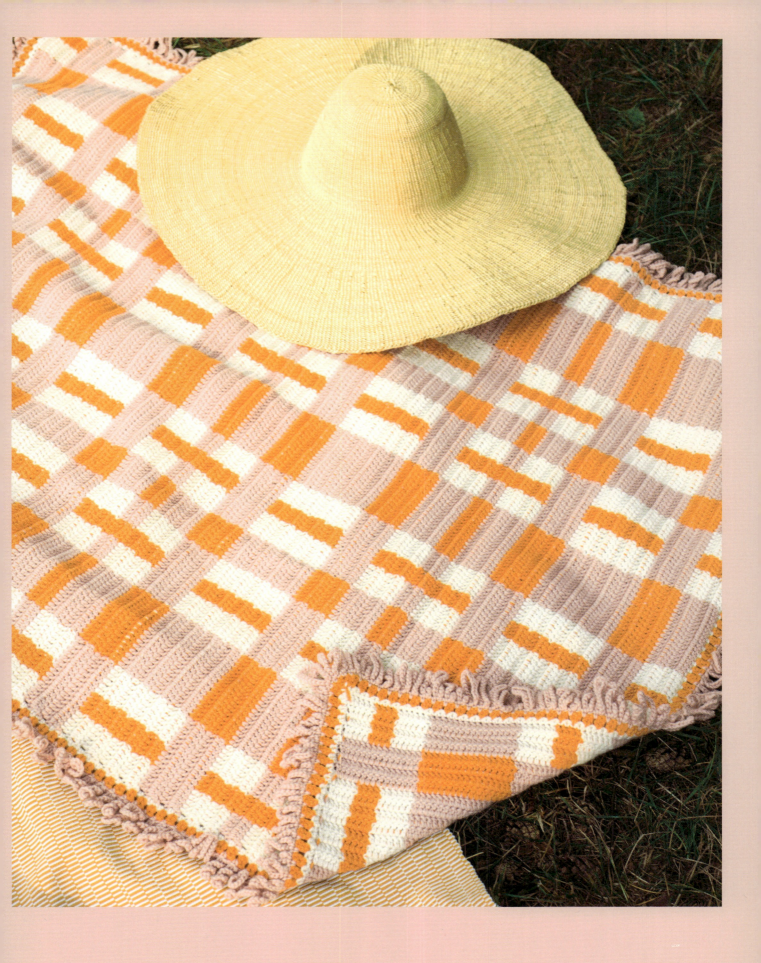

Aita blanket

SIZE	w. 90 cm, l. 110 cm (w. 35 in, l. 43 in) without border
YARN	Highland Yarn by Kit Couture (100% wool, 50 g roll = 100 m / 1 ¾ oz roll = 110 yd), orange 5 rolls, natural white 6 rolls, pink 10 rolls
HOOK	3.5 mm (E-4)
GAUGE	19 dc x 10 rows = 10 x 10 cm (4 x 4 in)

INFO

The blanket is worked back and forth in double crochet stitches, carrying the other yarns inside the stitches throughout the work. Make sure not to pull the carry-on yarns too tight, keep them loose. Leave the carry-on yarn one stitch from the end of each row to make sure the yarn loops will not show on the right side of the work. Change the colour of the yarn in the last yarn over of the stitch.

ABBREVIATIONS

ch = chain stitch
st = stitch
dc = double crochet stitch
sdc = starting double crochet stitch
sc = single crochet stitch
yoh = yarn over hook
sl st = slip stitch

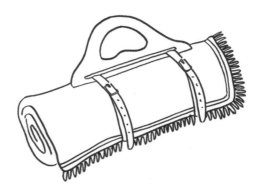

INSTRUCTIONS

Work 162 ch in natural white yarn to begin.

ROW 1. Work 1 dc in the fourth st from the hook, grab the other yarns in the work. Work *4 dc in natural white yarn, 4 dc in orange yarn, 6 dc in natural white yarn, 16 dc in pink yarn, 6 dc in natural white yarn, 4 dc in orange yarn, 6 dc in natural white yarn, 8 dc with pink yarn, 2 dc in natural white yarn*, repeat *–* altogether 3 times. *Hey! The last pattern repeat ends before the pink stripe.* Leave the carry-on yarns one st from the end at the backside of the work.

You have 160 dc in the row, which is 3 pattern repeats in width (work the third pattern repeat without the pink stripe). One pattern repeat is 56 dc in width and 26 rows in height.

ROWS 2–4. Work 2 ch in natural white yarn, as this is the first dc of each row. Grab the other yarns in the work. Work the rows as for row 1. *Hey! Since the next row starts with pink yarn, change the colour of the yarn in the last yoh.*

ROW 5. Work 2 ch in pink yarn, grab the other yarns in the work. Work *15 dc in pink yarn, 16 dc in orange yarn, 16 dc in pink yarn, 8 dc in orange yarn, 1 dc in pink yarn*, repeat *–* altogether 3 times. Leave the carry-on yarns one st from the end at the backside of the work.

ROWS 6–102. Work altogether 102 rows (4 vertical pattern repeats, the last two rows are not worked).

Continue the work without cutting the yarns.

BORDER

SINGLE CROCHET ROUND. Start with natural white yarn at the top right corner of the blanket. Work 1 ch and 1 sc in the same st. Work 1 sc in each st, in the corner, work 3 sc in the same st, on both sides work 2 sc in each row. Close round with a sl st. Cut yarn and weave in ends.

DOUBLE CROCHET ROUND. Change to orange yarn, continue at the top right corner of the blanket. Work a sdc, work 2 dc in the next st. *Skip 1 st and work 2 dc in the next st*, repeat *–* in all four sides of the work. In the corners, work 2 dc, 1 dc, 2 dc without skipping sts. Cut yarn and weave in ends.

FRINGE. Change to pink yarn, continue at the top right corner of the blanket. Work 1 ch, work 20 ch and close the first pink fringe with a sl st in the first of 20 ch sts. Work 1 sc in between the next two dc, work another 20 ch fringe and close it with a sl st in the first ch, work 1 sc in between the next two dc. Work *20 ch, close with a sl st, 1 ch, 1 sc*, repeat *–* in all four sides of the work. In all five corner sts, work a 20 ch fringe without ch sts.
Cut yarns and weave in ends.

Aita

Chart

Pattern repeat w. 56 sts, h. 26 sts

Double crochet stitch, dc

Aita

Pattern repeat w. 56 sts, h. 26 sts

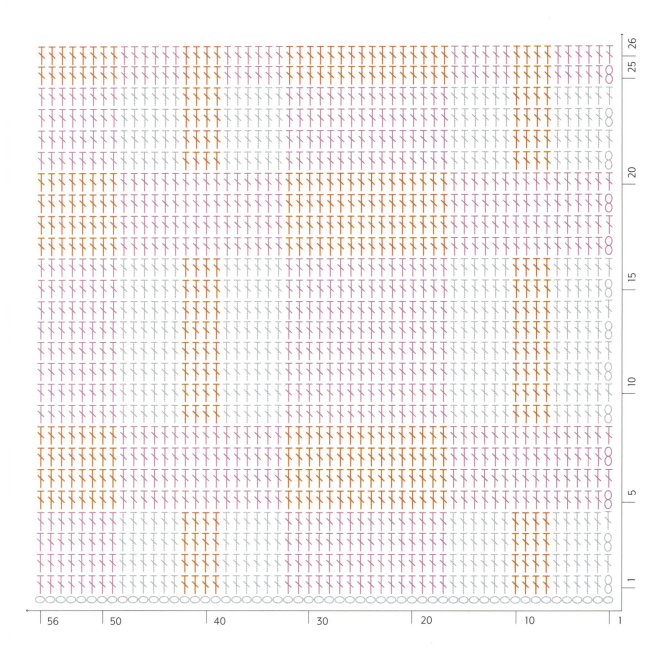

Chart, border

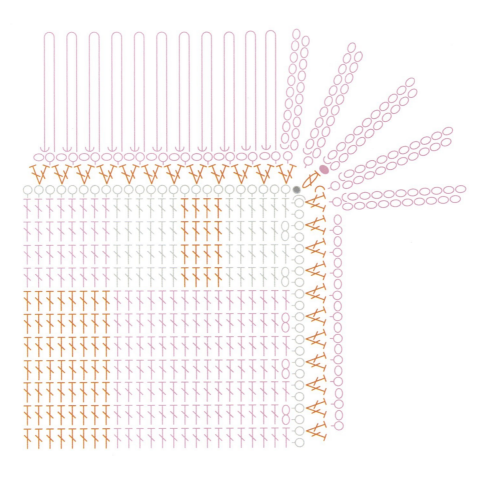

starting double crochet stitch, sdc	20 ch sts
double crochet stitch, dc	
chain, ch	
single crochet stitch, sc	
increase, 2 dc worked in a same st	
first st of the round	
slip stitch, sl st	

Linja

By making everyday items yourself, you can be sure of their sustainability. Choose an extra durable material for your project – such as the high-quality cotton twine used for this shopper – and you are guaranteed to use the finished piece for almost an eternity.

I had been working on an idea for a while: a crocheted shopper that would have a similar shape to a plastic shopping bag. It had been on my mind while wading through a raft of plastic waste on the southern beach of Lantau Island, Hong Kong, while dumpster-diving in one of the plastic recycling bins in Hämeenlinna, Finland, and while watching how the sales assistant in my corner shop in Williamsburg used several plastic bags to pack the two bananas I had just purchased.

A crocheted shopper is a more sustainable and durable solution, and it is also much nicer to look at.

Linja shopper

SIZE	Brown bag: w. 32 cm (when folded in shape), h. 58 cm (including the handles) (w. 12 ½ in, h. 23 in)
YARN	Liina cotton twine, 18-ply, by Suomen Lanka (100% cotton, 500 g roll = 840 m / 1 lb 2 oz roll = 919 yd, Tex 30 x 18), natural white 350 g (12 ½ oz), Molla cotton twine, 18-ply, by Suomen Lanka, brown 350 g (12 ½ oz)
HOOK	2.25 mm (B-1)
GAUGE	12 dc x 6 rows = 5 x 5 cm (2 x 2 cm)

INFO

The shopper is worked back and forth in double crochet stitches, carrying the other yarn inside the stitches throughout the work. Make sure not to pull the carry-on yarn too tight, keep it loose. Leave the carry-on yarn one stitch from the end of each row to make sure the yarn loops will not show on the right side of the work. Change the colour of the yarn in the last yarn over of the stitch. Work two similar pieces and sew them together.

ABBREVIATIONS

ch = chain stitch
st = stitch
sc = single crochet
dc = double crochet
yoh = yarn over hook
sl st = slip stitch

INSTRUCTIONS

Work 124 chain stitches in natural white yarn to begin.

ROW 1. Work 1 dc in the fourth st from the hook, grab the brown yarn in the work. Work 7 dc in natural white yarn, change to brown yarn in the last yoh. Work *8 dc in brown yarn, 8 dc in natural white yarn*, repeat *–* altogether 7 times. In the last st, work 1 dc in natural white yarn. Leave the brown yarn one st from the end at the backside of the work.

There are now have 15 stripes in your work. The first and last stripe are 9 dc in width, the other stripes are 8 dc in width.

ROW 2. Work 3 ch, as this is the first dc of each row. Grab the brown yarn in the work, work *8 dc in natural white yarn, 8 dc in brown yarn*, repeat *–* until the end of the round. In the last st, work 1 dc in natural white yarn. Leave the brown yarn one st from the end at the backside of the work.

ROWS 3–43. Work as for row 1. Cut yarns and weave in ends.

HANDLES

ROW 44. Start from the backside of the work 7 sts from the end with natural white yarn. Work 3 ch, 1 dc in the next 2 sts, change to brown yarn in the last yoh. Work 8 dc in brown yarn, 8 dc in natural white yarn, 8 dc in brown yarn, 8 dc in natural white yarn. Work 2 dc in brown yarn, work the next 2 sts together (decrease). To decrease in dc, start two individual dc sts, you have 3 loops on the hook, yoh, pull through all loops on the hook.

ROW 45. Work 3 ch, 1 dc in the next 2 sts, change to natural white yarn in the last yoh. Work 8 dc in natural white yarn, 8 dc in brown yarn, 8 dc in natural white yarn, 8 dc in brown yarn. Change to natural white yarn, work the next 2 sts together.

ROW 46. Work 3 ch in natural white yarn, change to brown yarn. Work 8 dc in brown yarn, 8 dc in natural white yarn,

8 dc in brown yarn, 8 dc in natural white yarn. Change to brown yarn, work the next 2 sts together.

ROW 47. Work 3 ch in brown yarn, change to natural white yarn. Work 8 dc in natural white yarn, 8 dc in brown yarn, 8 dc in natural white yarn, 8 dc in brown yarn.

ROWS 48–65. Follow the pattern chart. Cut yarns and weave in ends.

Work another similar piece.

SEWING

Place the two pieces together right sides in, join the sides together with a single crochet seam leaving the seam inside the work. Turn the work right side out.

Fold both sides inwards leaving 2.5 stripes inside the work. Close the bottom (80 sts) with a single crochet seam. *Hey! This seam is going to be thick. You have four layers of work to join in the seam. Work the stitches in the front loop of each stitch.* The width of the shopper is now 9 full stripes and half a stripe on both sides.

Work the two handle seams with the same pattern. The width of one handle is 2 full stripes and a half, 21 sts.

Hey! You have lots of yarn tails to weave in in this work. To ease your task, leave long yarn tails whenever possible to use in the single crochet seams.

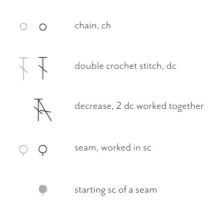

○	o	chain, ch
		double crochet stitch, dc
		decrease, 2 dc worked together
○	○	seam, worked in sc
●		starting sc of a seam

Chart

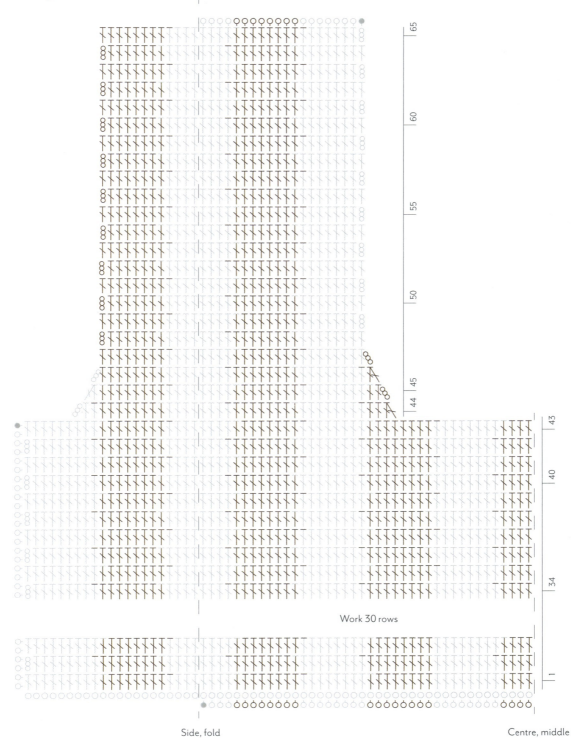

65

60

55

50

45

44 | 45

43

40

34

Work 30 rows

1

Side, fold

Centre, middle

LINJA PINK BAG is worked with the same pattern but with thin yarn, which makes the work naturally smaller.

SIZE w. 27 cm (when folded in shape), h. 43 cm
(w. 10 ¾ in, h. 16 ⁹/₁₀ in)
YARN Suomen Lanka Molla twine 12-ply
(100% cotton, 500 g roll = 1280 m / 1 lb 2 oz roll =
1400 yd, Tex 30 x 12),
rosa 180 g, Liina twine 12-ply, natural white 180 g (6 ½ oz)
HOOK 1.75 mm (US steel 6 / 7)
GAUGE 14 dc x 7 rows = 5 x 5 cm (2 x 2 in)

Kaari

When the night gets colder and Janis Joplin takes the stage at Woodstock, this is the shawl I wrap around my shoulders. The colours are taken straight from the Woodstock festival poster: purple and amber on a base of natural white. This crochet work is easy to carry with you on a work trip, on a tour or on a drive from New York City to Woodstock. On the two-hour ride there, you will get halfway through the shawl and finish the whole project before the gig that evening.

When you are choosing the colours for your crochet projects, I recommend you take a look at album covers and gig posters from different decades – there are some wild colour combos to choose from!

Kaari shawl

SIZE	w. 115 cm, l. 140 cm (w. 45 in, l. 55 in)
YARN	Highland Yarn by Kit Couture
	(100% wool, 50 g roll = 100 m / 1 ¾ oz
	roll = 109 yd), natural white 6 rolls, lilac
	3 rolls, orange 3 rolls
HOOK	4 mm (G-6)
GAUGE	15 dc x 9 rows = 10 x 10 cm (4 x 4 in)

INFO

The shawl is worked in double crochet stitches from right
to left at all rows. Cut the yarns after each row leaving
25 cm (10 in) long yarn tails for the tassels. When working
in two colours, carry the other yarn inside the stitches
throughout the row and make sure the carry-on yarn is not
too tight.

ABBREVIATIONS

ch = chain stitch
st = stitch
dc = double crochet stitch
sc = single crochet stitch
yoh = yarn over hook

INSTRUCTIONS

Work 230 chain stitches in natural white yarn to begin, leave a 25 cm (10 in) long yarn tail for the tassel.

ROW 1. Work 1 dc in the fourth st from the hook. Work 1 dc in each st. Leave a 25 cm (10 in) yarn tail, cut the yarn. You have 228 dc in the row including the ch sts in the beginning.

ROWS 2–8. Start from the right corner, work 1 dc in each st. Leave a 25 cm (10 in) long yarn tail at both ends of the row, cut the yarn.

ROW 9. Change to lilac yarn, grab the natural white in the work. Work 8 dc in lilac yarn, change to natural white yarn in the last yoh. Work *36 dc in natural white yarn, 8 dc in lilac yarn*, repeat *–* until the end of the row. Cut yarns.

You have 228 dc in the row, which is 5 pattern repeats and 8 dc continuing the pattern. One pattern repeat is 44 dc in width.

ROWS 10–42. Follow the pattern chart. Leave a 25 cm (10 in) long yarn tail at both ends of the row.

Work a single crochet st row in natural white yarn on both long sides of the work. Cut yarns.

Hey! Pull the work gently from the corners to make sure the carry-on yarns are not too tight inside the sts.

TASSELS

Cut 50 cm (19 ¾ in) long pieces of yarn in each colour. Weave one piece of yarn through each row on both ends of the work. Tie them on a knot together with the yarn tails you have left on each row.

Kaari

Chart

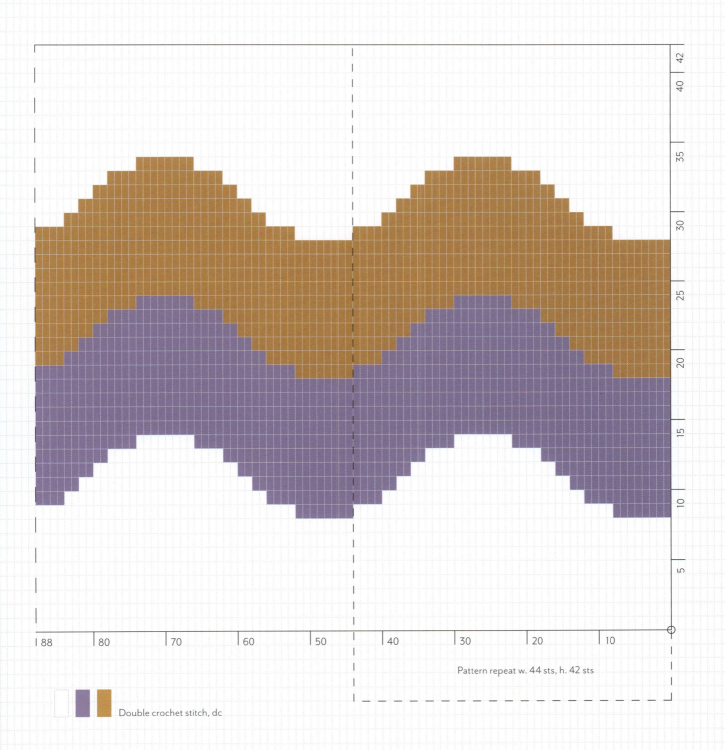

Pattern repeat w. 44 sts, h. 42 sts

Double crochet stitch, dc

Smile

The iconic yellow smiley face that we all know so well and use every day on social media was originally designed as a logo for an insurance company in the 1960s. The symbol is a depiction of the smile the other person would be able to see if the discussion was happening face to face. A smile is contagious – it illuminates your whole body from head to toe, and sometimes you can even hear it in a person's voice during a phone call.

The Smile shoulder bag is worked in squares, and while it takes some time, all the hours spent crocheting will definitely be worth it when you throw the bag over your shoulder. With this bag, you will brighten the day of every passer-by.

Smile shoulder bag

SIZE	w. 30 cm, h. 30 cm, d. 10 cm (w. 12 in, h. 12 in, d. 4 in) size of one square is 10 cm x 10 cm (4 x 4 in)
YARN	Liina cotton twine, 12-ply, by Suomen Lanka (100% cotton, 500 g roll = 1280 m / 1 lb 2 oz roll = 1400 yd, Tex 30 x 12), natural white 300 g (10 ½ oz). Molla cotton yarn, 12-ply, by Suomen Lanka (100% cotton, 500 g roll = 1280 m / 1 lb 2 oz roll = 1400 yd, Tex 30 x 12), yellow 100 g (3 ½ oz).
HOOK	1.75 mm (US steel 6 / 7)
OTHER	black embroidery yarn, cotton fabric for lining 80 x 40 cm (31 x 15 ¾ in)

INFO

Work 24 squares for the bag, join them together with slip stitches. Embroider a smiling face in the middle of the squares. Work a reinforcing border on the top of the bag, a separate base, and lastly, work two handles in single crochet stitches.

ABBREVIATIONS

rnd = round, rounds
ch = chain stitch
s = stitch
sc = single crochet stitch
dc = double crochet stitch
sdc = starting double crochet stitch
half-dc = half double crochet stitch
long-dc = long double crochet stitch
super-dc = super long double crochet stitch
yoh = yarn over hook
sl st = slip stitch

INSTRUCTIONS

SQUARE

RND 1. Roll a yarn loop around a finger with yellow yarn, close it with a sc, work 2 ch. Work 11 dc in the loop, carry the yarn tail inside the sts. Close round with a sl st. You now have 12 dc including the ch sts. To close the hole, pull the yarn tail tight.

RND 2. Work a sdc and 1 dc in the next st. Work 2 dc in each st, close all rounds with a sl st (24 dc).

RND 3. Work a sdc, work *2 dc in the next sts, 1 dc*, repeat *–* until the end of the round (36 dc).

RND 4. Work a sdc, work 1 dc, 2 dc in the next sts. *Work 1 dc, 1 dc, 2 dc in the next sts*, repeat *–* until the end of the round (48 dc).

RND 5. Work a sdc, work 1 dc in the next 2 sts. Work *2 dc in the next sts, 1 dc, 1 dc, 1 dc*, repeat *–* until the end of the round (60 dc).

Cut yellow yarn and weave in ends. Change to natural white yarn.

RND 6. Work a sdc, work *1 sc in the next 6 sts, 1 half-dc, 1 dc, 1 dc, 1 long-dc, 2 super-dc + 3 ch + 2 super-dc in the next sts, 1 long-dc, 1 dc, 1 dc, 1 half-dc*, repeat *–* in all four sides of the square. Close round with a sl st.

RND 7. Work a sdc, work 1 dc in the next 12 sts, work *2 dc + 3 ch + 2 dc in ch from the previous rnd, 1 dc in the next 18 sts*, repeat *–* in all four sides of the square.

RND 8. Work a sdc, work 1 dc in the next 14 sts, work *2 dc + 3 ch + 2 dc in ch from the previous rnd, work 1 dc in the next 22 sts*, repeat *–* in all four sides of the square.

Cut yarn and weave in ends.

Work altogether 24 squares with the same pattern. Embroider a smiling face in the middle of each square in black yarn. Block the squares in shape.

BASE

Work a bottom piece back and forth in single crochet stitches in natural white yarn.
Work 85 chain stitches in natural white yarn to begin.

ROW 1. Work 1 sc in the second st from the hook, work 1 sc in each st (84 sc).

ROW 2. Work 1 ch, work 1 sc in each st (84 sc).

ROWS 3–28. Work as for round 2. Cut yarn and weave in ends.

SEWING

Join the squares together with a slip stitch seam in natural white yarn. Place the first two squares side by side, work the sl sts in the back loop of each st. Put the hook through the middle st in the corner, take a yoh, pull through both layers. Then put the hook through the next sts, remember, back loop only, and continue working 29 more sl sts. When you reach the corner st, grab the next two squares in the work and continue the seam without cutting the yarn. Work the third pair of squares in the same seam, cut yarn.

Continue joining the squares together with the same pattern. The height of the bag is 3 squares and the width is 8 squares. *Hey! Work all squares together in vertical seams, then work two long horizontal seams to join all squares in one fabric.*

Join the base in the work with a sl st seam, or sew it in place by hand. Cut yarn and weave in ends.

BORDER

Work a reinforcing border at the top edge of the work in single crochet stitches in natural white yarn. Start from the top right corner.

RND 1. Work 1 sc. Work 1 sc in each st of the squares, skip the seams (8 squares x 28 sc = 224 sc).

RNDS 2–6. Work 1 sc in each st. Leave a 1,5 m long yarn tail for sewing, cut yarn.

Fold the border in two and sew the seam by hand.

HANDLES

Work two long handles back and forth in single crochet stitches.
Work 151 ch in natural white yarn to begin.

ROW 1. Work 1 sc in the second st from the hook, work 1 sc in each st (150 sc).

ROW 2. Work 1 ch, work 1 sc in each st (150 sc).

ROWS 3–6. Work as for row 2. Continue without cutting the yarn.

Join the long sides of both handles together with a slip stitch seam, this will give more years of use for the handles.

Attach the handles on the top edge of the bag inside the work by hand.

LINING

Cut a lining according to the size of your work. Sew the lining inside the work by hand.

Smile

Chart and embroidery pattern

○	starting loop
○ ○	chain, ch
♀ ♀	single crochet stitch, sc
Ѧ Ѧ	starting double crochet stitch, sdc
Ŧ Ŧ	double crochet stitch, dc
⊂ ⊂	slip stitch, sl st
V V	increase, 2 dc worked in a same st
⊤	half double crochet stitch, half-dc
Ŧ	long double crochet stitch, long-dc, 2 yoh
∦	super long double crochet stitch, super-dc, 3 yoh

Smile

Chart, top border, bottom and handles

Handles, fold

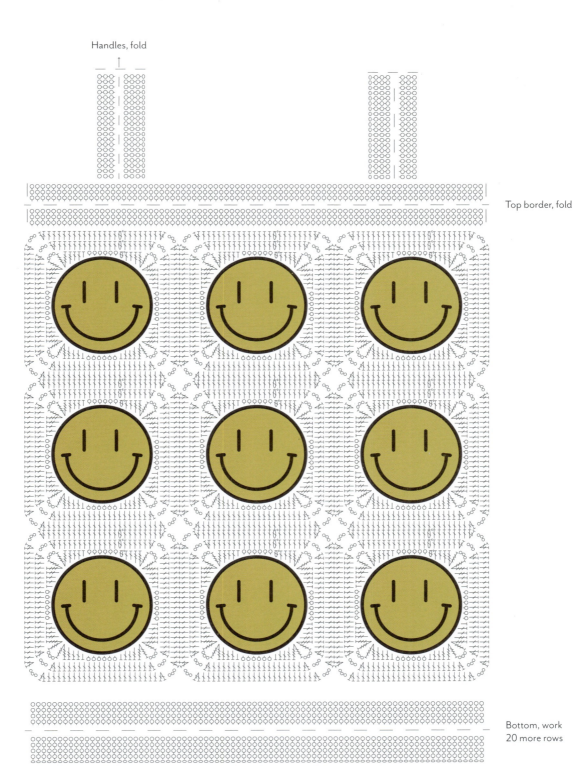

Top border, fold

Bottom, work
20 more rows

Loiva

It is important to take the time to take care of your mind and body. But even when you know this, it is always challenging to crawl out from under your warm blanket and on to the draughty floor to do your morning yoga asanas. I admire the will power of people who choose to practice yoga on a cold mattress instead of staying in the warmth of one's bed and who take a cold shower instead of a warm bath.

The first of these problems is easily fixed with a crocheted, woollen yoga mattress that is so warm your body doesn't even notice having left that cosy blanket behind. Roll the woollen mattress up to take with you on a camping trip, and also crochet a cushion with the same pattern to carry with you.

Loiva mattress

SIZE	w. 55 cm, l. 110 cm (w. 22 in, l. 43 in)
YARN	Muhku Wool by Lankava (100% wool, 1 kg roll = 390 m / 2 lb 3 oz roll = 426 yd, Tex 850 x 3), black 2 kg (4 lb 6 oz), natural white 1.5 kg (3 lb 5 oz)
HOOK	7 mm (K-10 ½ / L-11)
GAUGE	10 dc x 5 rnds = 10 x 10 cm (4 x 4 in)
OTHER	4 buttons and thin leather cord to attach the buttons, inner mattress 55 x 110 cm (22 x 43 in)

INFO

The mattress is worked in closed rounds in double crochet stitches, carrying the other yarn inside the stitches throughout the work. Make sure not to pull the carry-on yarn too tight, keep it loose. Change the colour of the yarn in the last yarn over of the stitch.

ABBREVIATIONS

rnds = round, rounds
ch = chain stitch
s = stitch
sdc = starting double crochet stitch
dc = double crochet stitch
sc = single crochet stitch
yoh = yarn over wool
sl st = slip stitch

INSTRUCTIONS

Work 114 chain stitches in natural white yarn to begin, join ring with a slip stitch.

RND 1. Work a sdc, grab the black yarn in the work, work 4 dc, change to black yarn in the last yoh. Work 12 dc in black yarn, 6 dc in natural white yarn, 12 dc in black yarn, 6 dc in natural white yarn, 12 dc in black yarn, 9 dc in natural white yarn, 12 sc in black yarn, 6 dc in natural white yarn, 12 dc in black yarn, 6 dc in natural white yarn, 12 dc in black yarn, 4 dc in natural white yarn. *Hey! Did you notice that on both sides of the work you crochet 9 dc in natural white instead of 6 dc?* Close round with a sl st on top of sdc.

You have 114 dc in the round, which is 6 pattern repeats + 6 dc. One pattern repeat is 18 dc in width and 10 rounds in height.

RND 2. Work a sdc with natural white yarn, grab the black yarn in the work, work 3 dc, change to black yarn in the last yoh. Work 12 dc in black yarn, 6 dc in natural white yarn, 12 dc in black yarn, 6 dc in natural white yarn, 12 dc in black yarn, 9 dc in natural white yarn, 12 sc in black yarn, 6 dc in natural white yarn, 12 dc in black yarn, 6 dc in natural white yarn, 12 dc in black yarn, 5 dc in natural white yarn. Close round with a sl st on top of sdc.

RNDS 3–57. Work altogether 57 rounds (6 vertical pattern repeats, the last 3 rounds are not worked).

TOP EDGE SEAM

Close the top edge of the work with a seam of single crochet stitches. Align the pattern repeats, start from the right corner with natural white yarn. Work 1 ch, grab the black yarn in the work. Put the hook through both layers and work 6 sc in natural white yarn, 12 sc in black yarn, 6 sc in natural white yarn, 12 sc in black yarn, 6 sc in natural white yarn, 12 sc in black yarn, 4 sc in natural white yarn. Cut yarns and weave in ends.

BUTTONHOLES

Work three single crochet rounds at the bottom edge of the work with natural white yarn, leaving holes for the buttons.

RND 1. Start from the bottom right corner, work 1 ch, work 1 sc in each st. Continue to the second round in a spiral.

RND 2. Work 1 sc in the next 62 sts, work a buttonhole: work *2 ch, skip 2 sts, work 1 sc in the next 13 sts*, repeat *–* until the end of the round. At the end of the round, work 5 sc instead of 13 sts.

RND 3. Work 1 sc in each sts.

Cut yarn and weave in ends. Measure places for the buttons, attach the buttons in place inside the work with a thin leather cord.

Loiva

Chart

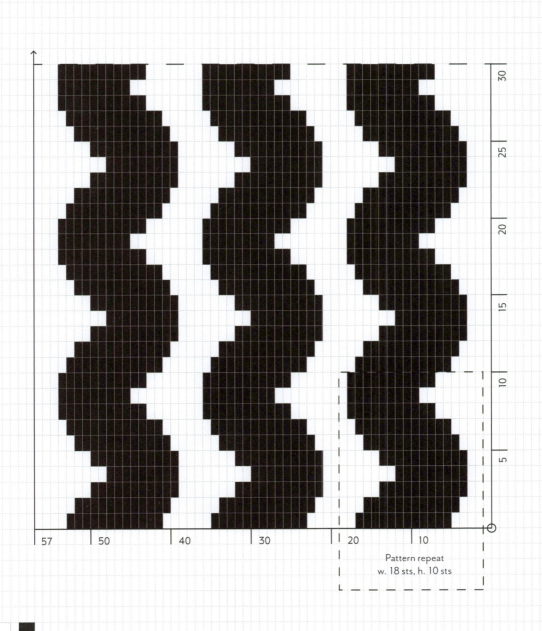

57   50   40   30   20   10

Pattern repeat
w. 18 sts, h. 10 sts

Double crochet stitch, dc

LOIVA CUSHION Work the cushion in a modified Loiva mattress pattern. The cushion is worked back and forth in single crochet stitches. To change a double crochet pattern into a single crochet pattern, simply work 2 stacked sc as in 1 dc.

The width of the cushion is 114 sc and the full length is 102 rows.

Fold the work in two and close three sides with a seam of single crochet stitches. Before closing, put the inner cushion inside the work. Cut yarns and weave in ends. Attach short leather handles on both sides of the work.

SIZE w. 70 cm, h. 35 cm (w. 27 ½ in, h. 13 ¾ in)

YARN Prato Cotton by Bettaknit (100% recycled cotton, 100 g skein = 100 m / 3 ½ oz skein =109 yd), black 6 skeins, natural white 5 skeins

HOOK 4 mm (G-6)

GAUGE 8 sc x 8 rows = 5 x 5 cm (2 x 2 in)

OTHER thin leather handles, inner cushion 70 x 35 cm (27 ½ in x 13 ¾ in)

Vasu

When I first saw pottery with impressions of textile fabrics at the Smithsonian in New York, I fell instantly in love! The use of linen fabric as a decorative tool had created a whole new dimension for the terracotta objects. By using stamps and knotted fabrics, a fabric-like texture is created on the clay surface.

The knit-like surface on the Vasu flower basket also looks to have been made when the potter was leaning on a drying clay pot with their sturdy woollen sweater. The basket is crocheted in a thick yarn, with robust knit stitches in a burnt terracotta colour. The top edge features a curvy pattern inspired by Portuguese tile designs.

Vasu basket

SIZE	cir. 90 cm (on top), 78 cm (on bottom), h. 14 cm / cir. 35 in (on top), 31 in (on bottom), h. 5 ½ in
YARN	Moppari mop yarn by Suomen Lanka (80% recycled cotton, 20% polyester, 1 kg roll = 310 m / 2 lb 3 oz roll = 339 yd, Tex 100 x 10 x 3), brown 500 g (1 lb 2oz), natural white 200 g (7 oz)
HOOK	6 mm (J-10)
GAUGE	5 sc x 6 rows = 5 x 5 cm (2 x 2 in)

INFO

Work the basket in rounds in two different stitches: single crochet stitches and knit stitches. In a single crochet stitch, take the yarn over through the top two yarn loops of the stitch. Put the hook through the whole stitch in a knit stitch, leaving the top two yarn loops and the back loop on top of the hook. Knit stitches are more robust than single crochet stitches, use an ergonomic hook to make them. Carry the other yarn in the work throughout the work.

ABBREVIATIONS

rnd = round, rounds
ch = chain stitch
st = stitch
sc = single crochet
kst = knit stitch
sl st = slip stitch

INSTRUCTIONS

BASE

Work 15 chain stitches in brown yarn to begin.

RND 1. Work 3 sc in the second st from the hook, grab natural white yarn in the work. Work 1 sc in the next 12 sts. Work 5 sc in the last st, turn and work 1 sc in the following 12 sts in the other edge of the foundation chain. Work 2 sc in the last st (you have 5 sc in both ends). Close all rounds with a sl st, leave carry-on yarn out of the sl st.

RND 2. Work 2 ch and 1 sc in the same st, grab the natural white yarn in the work, work 2 sc in the next 2 sts, 1 sc in the next 12 sts. In the corner, work 2 sc in the next 5 sts. Work 1 sc in the next 12 sts, work 2 sc in the next 2 sts (44 sc).

RND 3. Work 2 ch, grab the natural white yarn in the work, work 1 sc. Work 2 sc in the next st, 1 sc, 2 sc in the next st, 1 sc in the next 14 sts. In the corner, work 2 sc in the next st, 1 sc, 2 sc in the next st, 1 sc, 1 sc, 2 sc in the next st, 1 sc, 2 sc in the next st. Work 1 sc in the next 14 sts, work 2 sc in the next st, 1 sc, 2 sc in the next st (52 sc).

RND 4. Work 2 ch, work 1 sc in each st (52 sc).

RND 5. Work 2 ch, work 1 sc in the next 3 sts. Work 2 sc in the next st, 1 sc, 1 sc, 2 sc in the next st, 1 sc in the next 14 sts, 2 sc in the next st, 1 sc, 1 sc, 2 sc in the next st, 1 sc in the next 4 sts, 2 sc in the next st, 1 sc, 1 sc, 2 sc in the next st, 1 sc in the next 14 sts. Work 2 sc in the next st, 1 sc, 1 sc, 2 sc in the next st (60 sc).

RND 6. Work 2 ch, work 1 sc in the next 3 sts. Work 2 sc in the next st, 1 sc, 1 sc, 2 sc in the next st, 1 sc in the next 18 sts, 2 sc in the same st, 1 sc, 1 sc, 2 sc in the same st, 1 sc in the next 4 sts, 2 sc in the next st, 1 sc, 1 sc, 2 sc in the next st, 1 sc in the next 18 sts. Work 2 sc in the next st, 1 sc, 1 sc, 2 sc in the same st (68 sc).

RND 7. Work 2 ch, work 1 sc in the next 3 sts. Work 2 sc in the next st, 1 sc, 1 sc, 2 sc in the next st, 1 sc, 1 sc, 2 sc in the next st, 1 sc in the next 16 sts, 2 sc in the next st, 1 sc, 1 sc, 2 sc in the next st, 1 sc, 1 sc, 2 sc in the next st, 1 sc in the next 4 sts, 2 sc in the next st, 1 sc, 1 sc, 2 sc in the next st, 1 sc, 1 sc, 2 sc in the next st, 1 sc in the next 16 sts. Work 2 sc in the next st, 1 sc, 1 sc, 2 sc in the next st, 1 sc, 1 sc, 2 sc in the next st (80 sc).

RND 8. Work 1 ch, work 1 sc in each st. *Hey! In this round, work the stitches on the stitch's back loop, leaving the other loop of the stitch on the right side of the work.*

BASKET

Continue the work in knit stitches, carry the other yarn in the work. From this on, work in a spiral without a visible seam. Use a stitch marker when changing the round. *Hey! When you work in a spiral, a small change of pattern will appear every time you change the round if you work in two or more colours.*

RNDS 9–10. Work 1 kst in each st.

RND 11. Work 6 kst, work 2 kst in the next st, 1 kst in the next 30 sts, 2 kst in the next st, 1 kst in the next 8 sts, 2 kst in the next st, 1 kst in the next 30 sts, 2 kst in the next st, 1 kst in the next 2 sts (84 kst).

RNDS 12–13. Work 1 kst in each st.

RND 14. Work 5 kst, work 2 kst in the next st, 1 kst in the next 34 sts, 2 kst in the next st, 1 kst in the next 6 sts, 2 kst in the next st, 1 kst in the next 34 sts, 2 kst in the next st, 1 kst (88 kst).

RND 15. Work 1 kst in each st.

RND 16. Pattern begins. Work 4 kst in brown yarn, change to natural white yarn in the last yoh. Work *6 kst in natural white yarn, 5 kst in brown yarn*, repeat *–* altogether 8 times. Work 1 sc in brown yarn.

RND 17. Work 3 kst in brown yarn, change to natural white yarn in the last yoh. Work *8 kst in natural white yarn, 3 kst in brown yarn*, repeat *–* altogether 8 times.

RND 18. Work 2 kst in brown yarn, change to natural white yarn in the last yoh. Work *10 kst in natural white yarn, 1 kst in brown yarn*, repeat *–* altogether 8 times.

RND 19. Work 1 kst in the next 4 sts in natural white yarn, 2 kst in the next st, 1 kst in the next 38 sts, 2 kst in the same st, 1 kst in the next 4 sts, 2 kst in the next st, 1 kst in the next 38 sts, 1 kst in the next 2 sts (92 kst).

RNDS 20–21. Work 1 sc in each st with natural white yarn.

Cut brown yarn and weave in ends. Work a slip stitch round with natural white yarn, cut yarn and weave in ends.

Vasu

Chart

Basket, circumference, bottom 80 kst,
top 92 kst

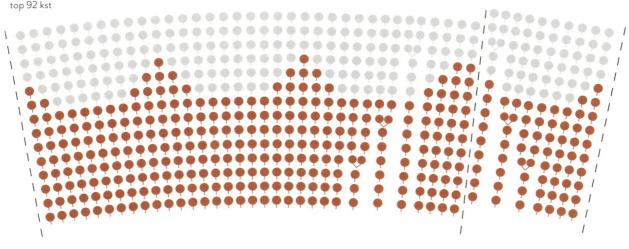

Round change point

Base, circumference 80 sc

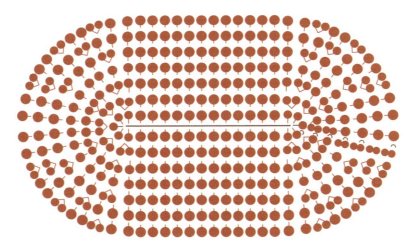

 foundation chain

single crochet stitch, sc (base),
knit stitch, kst (basket)

 slip stitch, sl st

increase, 2 sc worked in a same st (base),
increase, 2 kst worked in a same st (basket)

Raita

It might look like a tiny Fiat, but the inside matches a family-size Volvo. The Raita shoulder bag is a great example of good planning that allows you to fit a lot into a small space. Sounds like a maker's workroom, doesn't it? Here the secret is the rounded sides, which allow for more space as well as create a beautiful shape.

You can fit everything in this bag that you need during the day: notebooks, a packed lunch, your crochet work-in-progress. You should also see how the Raita shoulder bag would look crocheted with a thinner yarn.

Raita shoulder bag

SIZE	w. 20 cm, h. 20 cm, d. 10 cm (w. 8 in, h. 8 in, d. 4 in)
YARN	Varppi twine by Suomen Lanka (100% cotton, 500 g roll = 500 m / 1 lb 2 oz roll = 547 yd, Tex 50 x 18), black 200 g (7 oz), natural white 200 g (7 oz)
HOOK	3.5 mm (E-4)
GAUGE	9 sc x 10 rows = 5 x 5 cm (2 x 2 in)
OTHER	leather strap, 2 openable metal rings d. 25 mm (1 in), 2 snap hooks, tuck lock

INFO

The bag is worked back and forth in single crochet stitches, with one colour at a time. To make the arched shape, add stitches evenly throughout the work. Make one big bag piece and two small side pieces. Join them together with a single crochet seam.

ABBREVIATIONS

ch = chain stitch
st = stitch
sc = single crochet
sl st = slip stitch

INSTRUCTIONS

LONG PIECE

Work 82 chain stitches in natural white yarn to begin.

ROW 1. Work 1 sc in the second st from the hook, work 1 sc in the next 79 sts. Work 3 sc in the last st, turn, work 1 sc in the next 80 sts in the other edge of the foundation chain. You have 163 sc in the round. Cut yarn.

ROW 2. Turn, change to black yarn, work 1 sc in the next 80 sts. At the same time, fasten off the natural white yarn tail inside the sts. In the corner, work 2 sc, 3 sc, 2 sc. Work 1 sc in the next 80 sts.

ROW 3. Turn, work 1 ch. Work 1 sc in the next 79 sts. In the corner, work 2 sc, 1 sc, 2 sc, 2 sc, 2 sc, 1 sc, 2 sc. Work 1 sc in the next 80 sts. Cut yarn.

ROW 4. Turn, change to white yarn. Work 1 sc in the next 81 sts. At the same time, fasten off the black yarn tail inside the sts. In the corner, work 2 sc, 1 sc, 2 sc, 1 sc, 2 sc, 2 sc, 1 sc, 2 sc, 1 sc, 2 sc. Work 1 sc in the next 81 sts.

ROW 5. Turn, work 1 ch, work 1 sc in each st. Cut yarn.

ROW 6. Turn, change to black yarn. Work 1 sc in the next 81 sts. At the same time, fasten off the natural white yarn tail inside the sts. In the corner, work 2 sc, 1 sc, 1 sc, 2 sc, 1 sc, 1 sc, 2 sc, 1 sc, 1 sc, 2 sc, 1 sc, 1 sc, 2 sc, 1 sc, 1 sc, 2 sc. Work 1 sc in the next 81 sts.

ROW 7. Turn, work 1 ch, work 1 sc in each st. Cut yarn.

ROW 8. Turn, change to natural white yarn. Work 1 sc in the next 86 sts. At the same time, fasten off the black yarn tail inside the sts. In the corner, work; 2 sc, 1 sc, 1 sc, 1 sc, 2 sc, 1 sc, 1 sc, 2 sc, 1 sc, 1 sc, 1 sc, 2 sc. Work 1 sc in the next 86 sts.

ROW 9. Turn, work 1 ch, work 1 sc in each st. Cut yarn.

ROW 10. Turn, change to black yarn. Work 1 sc in the next 86 sts. At the same time, fasten off the natural white yarn tail inside the sts. In the corner, work 2 sc, 1 sc, 1 sc, 2 sc, 1 sc, 1 sc, 2 sc, 1 sc, 1 sc, 2 sc, 1 sc, 1 sc, 2 sc. Work 1 sc in the next 86 sts.

ROW 11. Turn, work 1 ch, work 1 sc in each st. Cut yarn.

ROW 12. Turn, change to natural white yarn. Work 1 sc in the next 89 sts. At the same time, fasten off the black yarn tail inside the sts. In the corner, work 2 sc, 1 sc, 1 sc, 1 sc, 2 sc, 1 sc, 1 sc, 1 sc, 1 sc, 1 sc, 1 sc, 2 sc, 1 sc, 1 sc, 1 sc, 2 sc. Work 1 sc in the next 89 sts.

ROW 13. Turn, work 1 ch, work 1 sc in each st. Cut yarn.

ROW 14. Turn, change to black yarn. Work 1 sc in the next 92 s:n. At the same time, fasten off the natural white yarn tail inside the sts. In the corner, work 2 sc, 1 sc, 1 sc, 1 sc, 2 sc, 1 sc, 1 sc, 1 sc, 1 sc, 2 sc, 1 sc, 1 sc, 1 sc, 2 sc. Work 1 sc in the next 92 sts.

ROW 15. Turn, work 1 ch, work 1 sc in each st. Cut yarn.

ROW 16. Turn, change to natural white yarn. Work 1 sc in the next 86 sts. At the same time, fasten off the black yarn tail inside the sts. Work 2 sc, 1 sc in the next 28 sts, 2 sc. Work 1 sc in the next 86 sts.

ROW 17. Turn, work 1 ch, work 1 sc in each st. Cut yarn.

ROW 18. Turn, change to black yarn. Work 1 sc in the next 87 sts. At the same time, fasten off the natural white yarn tail inside the sts. In the corner, work 2 sc, 1 sc, 1 sc, 1 sc, 1 sc, 2 sc, 1 sc, 1 sc, 1 sc, 1 sc, 2 sc, 1 sc, 1 sc, 1 sc, 1 sc, 1 sc, 2 sc, 1 sc, 1 sc, 1 sc, 1 sc, 1 sc, 2 sc, 1 sc, 1 sc, 1 sc, 1 sc, 2 sc. Work 1 sc in the next 87 sts.

ROW 19. Turn, work 1 ch, work 1 sc in each st. Cut yarn.

ROW 20. Turn, change to natural white yarn. Work 1 sc in each st. At the same time, fasten off the black yarn tail inside the sts. Cut yarn and weave in ends.

SIDE PIECE

Work 24 chain stitches in natural white yarn to begin.

ROW 1. Work 1 sc in the second st from the hook. Work 1 sc in the next 21 sts. Work 3 sc in the last st, turn, work 1 sc in the next 22 sts in the other edge of the foundation chain. You have 47 sc in the row. Cut yarn.

ROW 2. Turn, change to black yarn. Work 1 sc in the next 21 sts. At the same time, fasten off the natural white yarn tail inside the sts. In the corner, work 2 sc, 3 sc, 2 sc. Work 1 sc in the next 22 sts.

ROW 3. Turn, work 1 ch. Work 1 sc in the next 21 sts. In the corner, work 2 sc, 1 sc, 2 sc, 2 sc, 2 sc, 1 sc, 2 sc. Work 1 sc in the next 22 sts. Cut yarn.

ROW 4. Turn, change to natural white yarn. Work 1 sc in the next 23 sts. At the same time, fasten off the black yarn tail inside the sts. In the corner, work 2 sc, 1 sc, 2 sc, 1 sc, 2 sc, 2 sc, 1 sc, 2 sc, 1 sc, 2 sc. Work 1 sc in the next 23 sts.

ROW 5. Turn, work 1 ch, work 1 sc in each st. Cut yarn.

ROW 6. Turn, change to black yarn. Work 1 sc in the next 23 sts. At the same time, fasten off the natural white yarn tail inside the sts. In the corner, work; 2 sc, 1 sc, 1 sc, 2 sc, 1 sc, 1 sc, 2 sc, 1 sc, 1 sc, 2 sc, 1 sc, 1 sc, 2 sc. Work 1 sc in the next 23 sts.

ROW 7. Turn, work 1 ch, work 1 sc in each st. Cut yarn.

ROW 8. Turn, change to natural white yarn. Work 1 sc in the next 28 sts. At the same time, fasten off the black yarn tail inside the sts. In the corner, work 2 sc, 1 sc, 1 sc, 1 sc, 2 sc, 1 sc, 1 sc, 2 sc, 1 sc, 1 sc, 1 sc, 2 sc. Work 1 sc in the next 28 sts. Cut yarn and weave in ends.

Work another similar piece.

SEWING

Place the small side piece under the long bag piece right sides out. Start from the right corner, put the hook through both layers, and join the pieces together with a single crochet seam. The seam is visible on the right side of the work.

Continue working single crochet stitches around the long bag piece, join the other side piece in the work. Cut yarn and weave in ends.

Attach the tuck lock in place. Attach the openable metal rings on top of the side pieces and sew the handle to the rings.

Raita

 Chart, side piece

1	3	5	7	8

 foundation chain

 chain, ch

single crochet stitch, sc

 increase, 2 sc worked in a same st

Chart, long piece

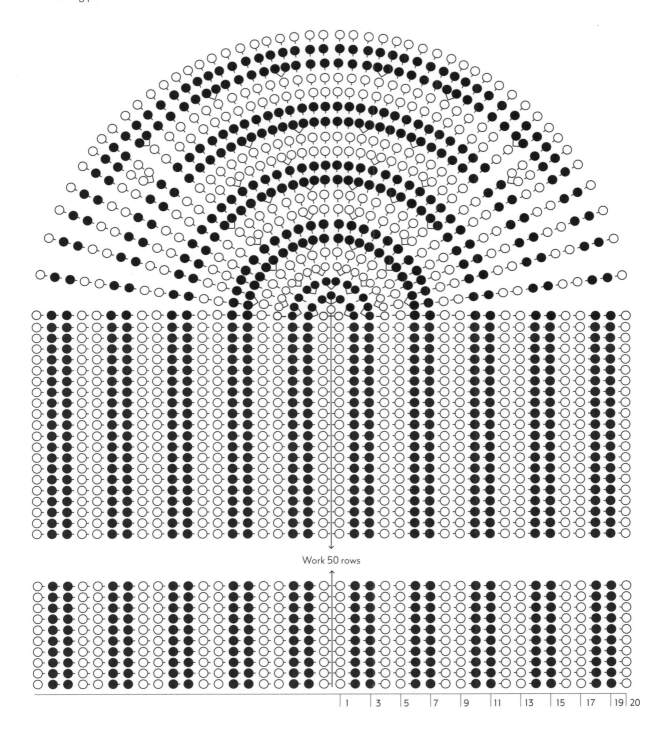

Work 50 rows

| 1 | 3 | 5 | 7 | 9 | 11 | 13 | 15 | 17 | 19 | 20 |

Raita shoulder bag can also be made with thin yarn.
Choosing a different yarn changes the size of the work.

Keto

This pattern is familiar, evoking many precious memories. You might have come across it in a picture book about 1970s German vinyl wallpapers or in a hardware store that still sells those retro vinyl floor coverings. These simple, clear patterns leave a permanent imprint, in a similar way to smells from important moments in our past.

My memory of this pattern is from a bathroom in Laihia, Finland, where the decor and the scent of Sunlight sauna soap created an unforgettable combo. The vinyl-covered walls made such an impression on this young maker that even many years later, the memory demanded to be turned into a crochet pattern. I've used the same pattern for a warming blanket, a cushion and a bag.

Keto blanket

SIZE	w. 115 cm, l. 140 cm (w. 45 in, l. 55 in)
YARN	Alpaca Brush by Bettaknit
	(44% alpaca, 44% wool, 12% polyamide,
	50 g roll = 200 m / 1 ¾ oz roll = 219 yd),
	brown 9 rolls, natural white 11 rolls
HOOK	7 mm (K-10 ½ / L-11)
GAUGE	10 sc x 10 rows = 10 x 10 cm (4 x 4 in)

INFO

The blanket is worked back and forth in single crochet stitches, carrying the other yarn inside the stitches throughout the work. Make sure not to pull the carry-on yarn too tight, keep it loose. Leave the carry-on yarn one stitch from the end of each row to make sure the yarn loops will not show on the right side of the work. Change the colour of the yarn in the last yarn over of the stitch.

ABBREVIATIONS

ch = chain stitch
st = stitch
sc = single crochet stitch
yoh = yarn over hook
sl st = slip stitch

INSTRUCTIONS

Work 131 chain stitches in natural white yarn to begin, leave a 7 m long yarn tail for the slip stitch row.

ROW 1. Work 1 sc in the second st from the hook, grab the brown yarn in the work. Work *15 sc, change to brown yarn in the last yoh, work 2 sc, change to natural white yarn in the last yoh, work 15 sc*, repeat *–* altogether 4 times. Leave the brown yarn one st from the end at the backside of the work.

You have 130 sc on the row, which is 4 pattern repeats and 2 sc sts on the right side of the work. One pattern repeat is 32 sc in width and 32 rows in height.

ROW 2. Work 1 ch in natural white yarn, as this is the first sc of each row. Grab the brown yarn in the work and work as for row 1.

ROW 3. Work 1 ch in natural white yarn, grab the brown yarn in the work. Work *2 sc in natural white yarn, 28 ch in brown yarn, 4 sc in natural white yarn*, repeat *–* altogether 4 times. At the end of the row, work 3 sc instead of 4 sc in natural white yarn.

ROW 4. Work 1 ch in natural white yarn, grab the brown yarn in the work. Work *1 sc, change to brown yarn, work 30 sc, change to natural white yarn, work 1 sc*, repeat *–* altogether 4 times. At the end of the row, work 2 sc instead of 3 sc in natural white yarn.

ROWS 5–162. Work altogether 162 rows (5 vertical pattern repeats and 2 rows on top according to the pattern).

Work a slip stitch row on both ends of the work in natural white yarn. Cut yarns and weave in ends.

Single crochet stitch, sc

Keto

Chart

Pattern repeat w. 32 sc, h, 32 rows

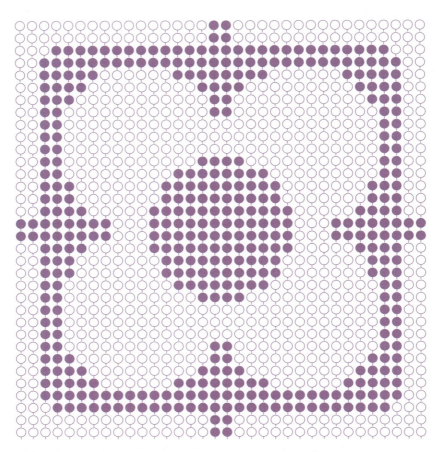

Keto pattern, detail from a chart.   ◯ ⬤ Single crochet stitch, sc

KETO CUSHION Work the cushion as for the blanket.
The width of the cushion is 66 sts (two pattern repeats
and I sc on each end according to the pattern), the height
is 66 rows.

Work two similar pieces, place them on top of each other
right sides out and crochet the three sides together with
single crochet stitches. Put the inner cushion inside and
close the fourth side with sc sts. Weave the thin leather
handle through the top seam of the work and tie it in place.

SIZE w. 45 cm, l. 45 cm
(w. 18 in, l. 18 in)
YARN Prato Cotton by Bettaknit
(100% recycled cotton, 100 g roll =
100 m / 3 ½ oz roll = 109 yd), lilac
4 skeins, natural white 7 skeins
HOOK 4.5 mm (US 7)
GAUGE 8 sc x 8 rows = 5 x 5 cm
(2 x 2 in)
OTHER 20 cm (8 in) long thin leather
strap for the handle, inner cushion
45 x 45 cm (18 x 18 in)

The width of the bag is 100 sc and the height is 98 rows. Work two similar pieces, sew a zipper on the backside of the work on the top opening, then sew a cotton ribbon on top of the zipper seam. Close the three sides with a sc seam in natural white yarn, cut yarn and weave in ends. Lastly, attach two leather handles on the bag.

SIZE w. 32 cm, l. 32 cm (w. 12 ½ in, l. 12 ½ in)
YARN Suomen Lanka Molla twine 12-ply
(100% cotton, 500 g roll = 840 m / 1 lb 2 oz roll = 918 yd, Tex 30 x 18), tomato red 200 g (7 oz), Liina twine 12-ply, natural white 200 g (7 oz)
HOOK 1.75 mm (US steel 6 / 7)
GAUGE 16 sc x 16 rows = 5 x 5 cm (2 x 2 in)
OTHER two thin leather straps 35 cm (13 ¾ in), zipper 30 cm (12 in), cotton ribbon 70 cm (27 ½ in)

Kannu

You can find vases, jugs and other domestic ceramics on the shelves of numerous museums. We often pass by these mundane-looking clay objects, but if we take time to stop and examine them more closely we can find traces of our ancestors' craftsmanship, of everyday life lived long ago. The curvy shape of each jug tells a story about the culture in which it was crafted and the beautiful patterns give great insight into past symbolism.

On your next museum visit, explore the shapes of the ceramics and then copy those shapes to your crochet works. You can crochet beautiful jugs just by increasing and decreasing stitches.

Kannu container

SIZE	h. 20 cm, d. 20 cm (h. 8 in, d. 8 in)
YARN	Moppari twisted mop yarn by Suomen Lanka (80% recycled cotton, 20% polyester, 1 kg roll = 310 m / 2 lb 3 oz roll = 339 yd, Tex 100 x 10 x 3), nude 550 g (1 lb 3 oz)
HOOK	6 mm (J-10)
GAUGE	5 kst x 6 rows = 5 x 5 cm (2 x 2 in)

INFO

Work the container in rounds starting from the bottom using two different stitches: single crochet stitches and knit stitches. In a single crochet stitch, take the yarn over through the top two yarn loops of the stitch. In a knit stitch, put the hook through the whole stitch leaving the top two yarn loops and the back loop on top of the hook. Knit stitches are more robust than single crochet stitches.

ABBREVIATIONS

rnd = round, rounds
ch = chain stitch
st = stitch
sc = single crochet
kst = knit stitch
sl st = slip stitch

INSTRUCTIONS

BASE

RND 1. Make a small yarn loop around a finger, work 10 sc in it. Carry the yarn tail inside the sts. To close the hole, pull the yarn tail tight. Continue to the second round in a spiral.

RND 2. Work 2 sc in each st (20 sc).

RND 3. Work 2 sc in every second st, work 1 sc in other sts (30 sc).

RND 4. Work 2 sc in every 3rd st, work 1 sc in other sts (40 sc).

RND 5. Work 1 sc in the two back loops of each st. This will form a visible seam on the right side of the work.

JAR

Knit stitch. Continue the work in knit stitches in rounds increasing and decreasing the stitches to give shape to the work.

RNDS 6–7. Work 1 kst in each st.

RND 8. Work 2 kst in every 5th st (increase), work 1 kst in other sts (48 kst).

RNDS 9–10. Work 1 kst in each st.

RND 11. Work 2 kst in every 6th st (increase), work 1 kst in other sts (56 kst).

RNDS 12–20. Work 1 kst in each st.

RND 21. Work every 5th and 6th st together (decrease), work 1 kst in other sts (47 kst).

RNDS 22–23. Work 1 kst in each sts.

RND 24. Work every 9th and 10th st together (decrease), work 1 st in other sts (43 kst).

RNDS 25–28. Work 1 kst in each st.

RND 29. Spout. Work 1 kst in the next 20 sts, work 2 kst in the next st, 1 kst, 2 kst in the next st. Work 1 kst in the next 20 sts.

RND 30. Work 1 kst in the next 21 sts, work 2 kst in the next 3 sts. Work 1 kst in the next 21 sts.

RND 31. Work 1 kst in each st.

Work a sl st round. Cut yarn and weave in ends.

Polku

This twisty, graffiti-like pattern is like something straight from the sunny streets of Wynwood, Miami. I could see this pattern decorating a trendy second-hand shop there, or as a bright orange, three-storeys-high mural, or in a rug such as this one.

After several failed crochet attempts, the Polku pattern slowly started to resemble the scrawls I had drawn in my sketch book that day in Wynwood. When I drew them, I was thinking about my own path, the one that had brought me there, to the hub of casinos and Cuban music – it was anything but straight.

The only way to walk across this rug is with your woollen socks on, following each curve of the winding path.

Polku rug

SIZE	w. 74 cm, l. 3 m (w. 29 in, l. 118 in)
YARN	Matilda yarn by Lankava (80% recycled cotton, 20% polyester, 500 g roll = 140 m / 1 lb 2 oz roll = 153 yd), black 8 rolls, natural white 11 rolls
HOOK	7 mm (K-10 ½ / L-11)
GAUGE	9 sc x 10 rows = 10 cm x 10 cm (4 x 4 in)

INFO

The rug is worked back and forth in single crochet stitches, carrying the other yarn inside the stitches throughout the work. Make sure not to pull the carry-on yarn too tight, keep it loose. Leave the carry-on yarn one stitch from the end of each row to make sure the yarn loops will not show on the right side of the work. Change the colour of the yarn in the last yarn over of the stitch.

ABBREVIATIONS

ch = chain stitch
st = stitch
sc = single crochet stitch
yoh = yarn over hook
sl st = slip stitch

INSTRUCTIONS

Work 68 chain stitches in natural white yarn to begin, leave a 3 m (118 in) long yarn tail for the slip stitch row.

ROW 1. Work 1 sc in the second st from the hook, grab the black yarn in the work. Work 5 sc, change to black yarn in the last yoh. Work 11 sc in black yarn, 11 sc in natural white yarn, 28 sc in black yarn, 11 sc in natural white yarn. Leave the black yarn one st from the end at the backside of the work.

You now have 67 sts, which is one full pattern repeat. One pattern repeat is 67 sc in width and 40 rows in height.

ROW 2. Work 1 ch in natural white yarn, as this is the first sc of each row, grab the black yarn in the work. Work 11 sc in natural white yarn, 28 sc in black yarn, 11 sc in natural white yarn, 10 sc in black yarn, 6 sc in natural white yarn.

ROWS 3–250. Follow the pattern chart. Work altogether 250 rows, which is 6 vertical pattern repeats and 10 more rows continuing the pattern.

Work a slip stitch row on both ends of the work in white yarn. Cut yarns and weave in ends.

Polku

Chart

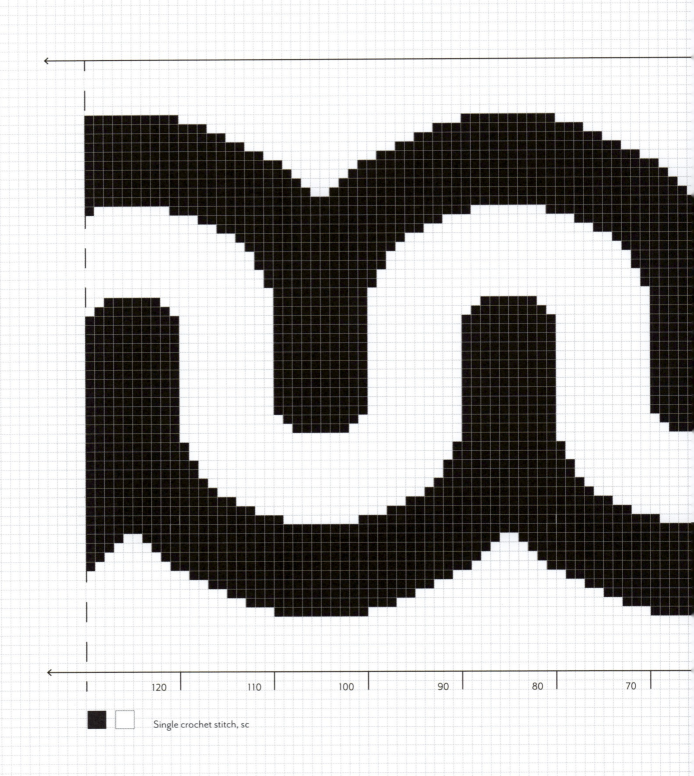

120	110	100	90	80	70

■ □ Single crochet stitch, sc

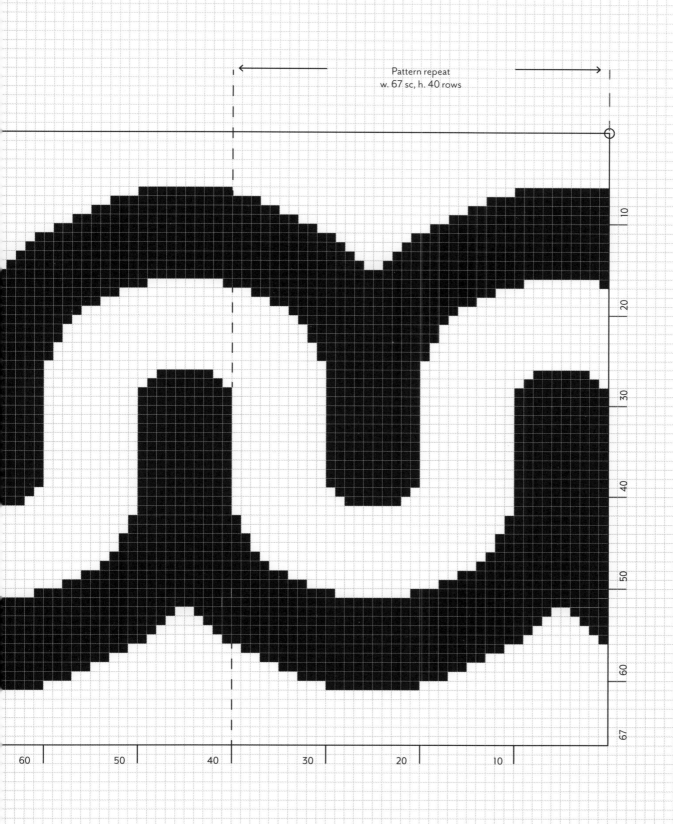

Pattern repeat
w. 67 sc, h. 40 rows

Ruutu

You can spot this square pattern everywhere: in the window frames of old houses, in those 1980s chequered pants, on the pages of your school notebook. My mother used this pattern in her weaving and made a tea cosy. Even industrially woven cross-stitch fabrics are based on the same square pattern.

Each maker tells their own story through their handcraft. In the process of making, the size, the purpose and even the material of the piece can change. Two beautiful things about handcrafts are convertibility and versatility — one simple pattern can be used in so many different works. This time, I have used this classic pattern to make a table mat and a mattress.

Ruutu table mat

SIZE	w. 35 cm (not including the paper yarn loops), h. 60 cm (w. 13 ¾ in, h. 23 ½ in)
YARN	Varppi twine by Suomen Lanka (100% cotton, 500 g roll = 500 m / 1 lb 2 oz roll = 547 yd, Tex 50 x 18), black 200 g (7 oz), natural white 200 g (7 oz). Filona flat paper ribbon, Lankava (100% paper, 100 g skein = 87 m / 14 oz skein = 95 yd, 0.80 Nm, Tex 1250), beige 100 g (14 oz).
HOOK	4 mm (G-6)
GAUGE	9 sc x 8 rows = 5 cm x 5 cm (2 x 2 in)

INFO

The table mat is worked back and forth in single crochet stitches, carrying the other yarn inside the stitches throughout the work. Carry the paper yarn inside the stitches in every second row. Make sure not to pull the carry-on yarn too tight, keep it loose. Leave the carry-on yarn one stitch from the end of each row to make sure the yarn loops will not show on the right side of the work. Change the colour of the yarn in the last yarn over of the stitch.

ABBREVIATIONS

ch = chain stitch

st = stitch

sc = single crochet

yoh = yarn over hook

sl st = slip stitch

INSTRUCTIONS

Cut the paper yarn in 3 m (118 in) long pieces, altogether 40 pieces, and fold in five to make 60 cm (23 ½ in) wide skeins.

Work 65 chain stitches in natural white yarn to begin, leave a 3 m (118 in) long yarn tail for the slip stitch row.

ROW 1. Work 1 sc in the second st from the hook, grab the black yarn in the work. Work 3 sc in natural white yarn, change to black yarn in the last yoh. Work *6 sc in black yarn, 4 sc in natural white yarn*. Repeat *–* altogether 6 times. Leave the black yarn one st from the end at the backside of the work.

You have 64 sc in the row, which is 6 pattern repeats and 4 sc continuing the pattern. One pattern repeat is 10 sc in width.

ROW 2. Work 1 ch in natural white yarn, as this is the first sc of each row. Grab the black yarn in the work, work as for row 1.

ROW 3. Grab a paper yarn skein in the work. Work 1 ch around the skein by taking the yoh under the skein and leaving 12 cm (4 ¾ in) long paper yarn tails on both ends of the row. Grab the black yarn in the work, work as for row 1, carry the paper yarn skein inside the sts throughout the row. *Hey! Since the paper yarn skein is rather thick, it makes every second row longer than the other rows. This is OK.* Leave the black yarn one st from the end at the backside of the work.

ROW 4. Work as for row 2.

ROWS 5–84. Follow the pattern chart. Carry the paper yarn skeins inside the sts in every second row.

Work a slip stitch row on both ends of the work. Cut yarns and weave in ends.

Ruutu

Chart

64	60	50	40	30	20	10

Pattern repeat
w. 10 sc

■□ Single crochet stitch, sc

RUUTU MATTRESS is made according to Ruutu table mat pattern. Instead of using a single crochet stitch as in Ruutu table mat, work the mattress in double crochet stitches. In this case, two overlapping sc stitches in the symbol chart are one dc. The circumference of the mattress is 120 dc and the height is 66 rounds. Work 120 chain sts in orange yarn to begin, close ring with a slip stitch. Grab along the natural white yarn, and follow the Ruutu symbol craft. Notice that the white pixels in the symbol craft are now orange and black pixels are natural white. Start each round of the mattress with a standing double crochet stitch (sdc).

Work altogether 66 rounds, close the bottom opening with sc seam in orange yarn. Place the inner cushions inside the work, and sew two horizontal seams by hand in between rounds 21/22 and rounds 43/44. This creates three cushion-like puffs in the mattress. Next, close the upper opening with sc seam in orange yarn. Place one leather handle in the middle of the bottom seam and the other handle in the middle of the top seam (between rounds 43/44).

SIZE w. 60 cm, h. 140 cm (w. 23 ½ in, h. 55 in)
YARN Lankava Muhku wool (100% wool, 1 kg roll = 390 m / 2 lb 3 oz roll = 426 yd, Tex 850 x 3), natural white 1.5 kg (3 lb 5 oz), orange 1.5 kg (3 lb 5 oz)
HOOK 7 mm (K-10 ½/L-11)
GAUGE 10 dc x 5 rnds = 10 x 10 cm (4 x 4 in)
OTHER two leather handles l. 35 cm (13 ¾ in), three inner cushions 60 x 45 cm (23 ½ x 18 in)

Puolikas

I always marvel at the geometric and colourful patterns of the 1960s! It was so easy to express your own bohemian personality by wearing a flowy Biba floral dress or an edgy, graphic Mary Quant jumpsuit. Fashion brought colour to everyday life and offered a chance to stand out. My wardrobe used to be filled with clothes made of bright green Terylene fabric and platform shoes, when the 2000s brought the style back for a brief while.

The Puolikas shoulder bag feels like travelling back in time to Swinging Sixties London, but looks equally stunning in today's setting as well.

Puolikas shoulder bag

SIZE	w. 18 cm, h. 15 cm, d. 7 cm (w. 7 in, h. 6 in, d. 2 ¾ in)
YARN	Liina twine, 12-ply, by Suomen Lanka (100% cotton, 500 g roll = 1280 m / 1 lb 2 oz roll = 1400 yd, Tex 30 x 12), black 150 g (5 ½ oz), natural white 150 g (5 ½ oz)
HOOK	1.75 mm (US steel 6 / 7)
GAUGE	15 sc x 15 rows = 5 cm x 5 cm (2 x 2 in)
OTHER	leather strap 1 m (39 in), 2 snap hooks, tuck lock

INFO

The bag is worked back and forth in single crochet stitches, carrying the other yarn inside the stitches throughout the work. Make sure not to pull the carry-on yarn too tight, keep it loose. Leave the carry-on yarn one stitch from the end of each row to make sure the yarn loops will not show on the right side of the work. Change the colour of the yarn in the last yarn over of the stitch. Work a separate bag and a lid, join them together with a slip stitch seam.

ABBREVIATIONS

ch = chain stitch
st = stitch
sc = single crochet
yoh = yarn over hook
sl st = slip stitch

INSTRUCTIONS

BAG

Work 83 chain stitches in natural white yarn to begin.

ROW 1. Work 1 sc in the second st from the hook, grab the black yarn in the work. *Hey! Work this row in the back loops of the foundation chain. This will reinforce the stitches.* Work *10 sc in natural white yarn, change to black yarn in the last yoh, and work 10 sc*, repeat *–*until the end of the row. Work 1 sc in black yarn, leave the natural white yarn one st from the end at the backside of the work.

You have 82 sc in the row, which is 4 pattern repeats and 1 sc on both sides. One pattern repeat is 20 sc in width and 20 rows in height.

ROW 2. Openings for the handles. Work 1 ch in black yarn, as this is the first sc of each row, work 5 sc. Then work an opening; work 4 sc around natural white yarn, skip 4 sts, work a sc in the following st. Work *10 sc in natural white yarn, 10 sc in black yarn*, repeat *–* altogether three times. Work 1 sc in natural white yarn, then work another opening for a handle. At the end of the row, work 6 sc in natural white yarn.

ROWS 3–4. Follow the pattern chart. Work altogether 104 rows, which is 5 vertical pattern repeats adding 2 rows on the bottom and top edge according to the pattern.

ROW 5. Work 1 ch. Work *7 sc in natural white yarn, 3 sc in black yarn, 3 sc in natural white yarn, 7 sc in black yarn*, repeat *–* altogether 4 times. At the end of the row, work 1 sc in black yarn.

ROWS 6–104. Follow the pattern chart. In row 103, work as for row 2 (openings for the handles). Cut yarns and weave in ends.

Puolikas

Chart, bag

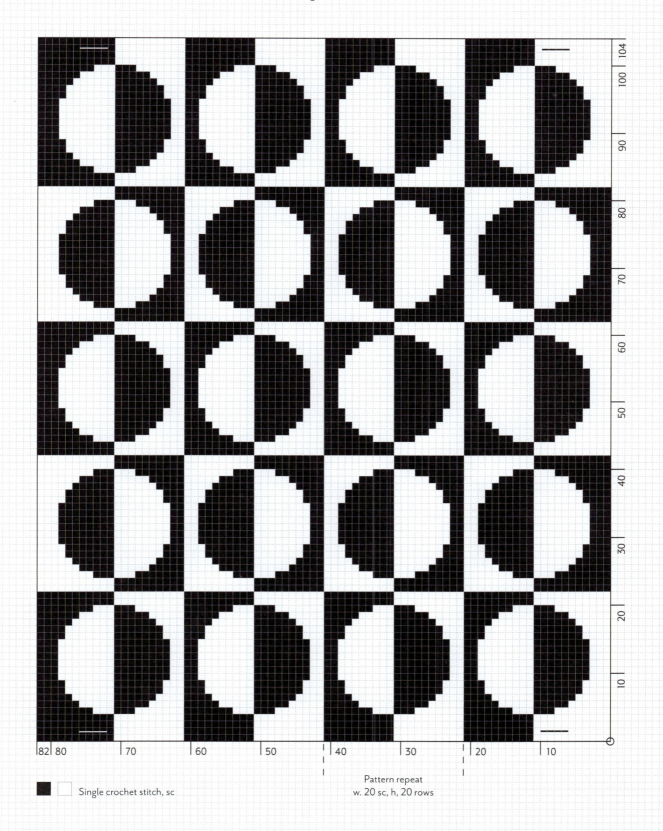

■ □ Single crochet stitch, sc

Pattern repeat
w. 20 sc, h, 20 rows

Puolikas

Chart, lid

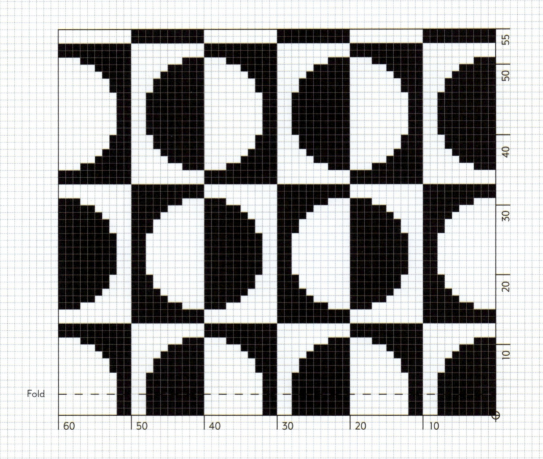

55
50
40
30
20
10
0

60   50   40   30   20   10

Fold

■ □ Single crochet stitch, sc

LID

Work 61 chain stitches in black yarn to begin.

ROW 1. Work 1 sc in the second st from the hook, grab the natural white yarn in the work. Work *7 sc in black yarn, change to natural white yarn in the last yoh, and work 2 sc. Continue working 2 sc in black yarn, 8 sc in natural white yarn, 1 sc in black yarn*, repeat *–*until the end of the row, the last black sc is not worked. Leave the black yarn one st from the end at the backside of the work.

You have 60 sc in the row, which is 3 pattern repeats (two full pattern repeats and a half of a repeat on both ends). One pattern repeat is 20 sc in width and 20 rows in height.

ROW 2. Work 1 ch natural white yarn, grab the black yarn in the work. Work *7 sc in natural white yarn, change to black yarn in the last yoh, and work 2 sc. Continue working 2 sc in natural white yarn, 8 sc in black yarn, 1 sc in natural white yarn*, repeat *–*until the end of the row, the last natural white sc is not worked.

ROWS 3–55. Follow the pattern chart. Work altogether 55 rows, which is 2 full pattern repeats adding 13 rows in the bottom and 2 rows in the top according to the pattern. Leave a 3 m long natural white yarn tail for sewing, cut black yarn and weave in ends.

SEWING

Fold the bag in two wrong sides out, sew side seams by hand leaving the seam allowance inside the work. Fold bottom corners inward in a triangle shape (to give volume for the bag) and sew a 7 cm (2 ¾ in) wide seam by hand. Turn the work right side out.

Fold three bottom rows of the lid inwards and sew a seam by hand. This folding will prevent the corners of the lid from rolling. Then pin the lid on the backside of the bag 8 rows from the top, sew in place by hand. *Hey! Maybe you noticed that the pattern of the lid does not match with the bag on the backside of the work, but on the right side it matches.*

Measure a place for the tuck lock and attach it in place.

Attach the snap hooks in the handle, and then weave the snap hooks through the openings on rows 2 and 103.

BIG PUOLIKAS TOTE BAG is made with the Puolikas shoulder bag pattern. The size of the tote bag is 82 sc and the height is 62 rows. Work two similar pieces, place them together right sides out and close the three sides with single crochet seam in both brown and natural white yarn. Sew a reinforcing cotton ribbon on top of the bag inside the work, then sew two leather handles in place.

SIZE w. 55 cm, h. 45 cm (w. 22 in, h. 18 in)

YARN Bettaknit Prato Cotton (100% recycled cotton, 100 g roll = 100 m / 3 ½ oz roll = 109 yd), brown 6 skeins, natural white 6 skeins

HOOK 4.5 mm (US 7)

GAUGE 8 sc x 8 rows = 5 x 5 cm (2 x 2 in)

OTHER two leather handles 50 cm (19 ¾ in), cotton ribbon 1.2 m (47 in)

Veska

My name was called out over the speakers at Helsinki Vantaa airport when I lost my small passport bag. Along with that bag, I had also lost my wallet, my keys, my tickets and my serenity. I had been so anxious about the trip ahead that I had hardly slept at all, and as a result my head was all over the place. The moment I put the passport bag down, I completely forgot it even existed.

I was saved by a fellow traveller who had found my treasures and as a result my name was now echoing from the walls of the terminal building. I could have avoided all the hassle and panic if I had placed my valuables into this bum bag instead – it is almost impossible to lose.

Veska bum bag

SIZE	w. 18 cm, h. 16 cm, d. 6 cm
	(w. 7 in, h. 6 ¼ in, d. 2 ½ in)
YARN	Rag yarn (cut 1 cm / ½ in wide strips
	from the rag), lilac 300 g (10 ½ oz).
	Thick cotton yarns also work for this piece.
HOOK	5 mm (H-8)
GAUGE	8 sc x 8 rnds = 5 x 5 cm (2 x 2 in)
OTHER	tuck lock, two leather pieces l. 4 cm
	(1 ½ in), leather belt

INFO

The bum bag is worked back and forth in single crochet stitches. Add stitches in two corners in each row and the work grows seamlessly. Make a separate front piece and back piece, a lid, and a pocket. Join them together with a slip stitch seam.

ABBREVIATIONS

ch = chain stitch
st = stitch
sc = single crochet
sl st = slip stitch

INSTRUCTIONS

FRONT PIECE

Work 12 chain stitches to begin.

ROW 1. Work 1 sc in the second st from the hook. Work 1 sc in the next 9 sts, 3 sc in the last st. Turn and work the sts on the other edge of the foundation chain. Work 1 sc in the next 10 sts, grab the yarn tail in the work and leave it inside the sts.

ROW 2. Turn, work 1 ch, work 1 sc in the next 9 sts. At the end of the row, work 2 sc in the same st, 3 sc in the next st, 2 sc in the next st. Work 1 sc in the next 10 sts.

ROW 3. Turn, work 1 ch, work 1 sc in the next 10 sts. At the end of the row, work 3 sc in the same st, 1 sc in the next 3 sts, 3 sc in the same st. Work 1 sc in the next 11 sts.

ROW 4. Turn, work 1 ch, work 1 sc in the next 11 sts. At the end of the row, work 3 sc in the same st, 1 sc in the next 5 sts, 3 sc in the same st. Work 1 sc in the next 12 sts.

ROWS 5–13. Follow the pattern chart. In each row work 3 sts in two corners.

ROW 14. Work as the other rows, but in the two corners, add 1 sc.

ROWS 15–22. Work sc rows.

Cut yarn and weave in ends.

BACK PIECE

Work the back piece as the front piece from row 1 to row 15. Leave a 3 m (118 in) long yarn tail for sewing, cut yarn.

POCKET

Work 9 chain stitches to begin. Work the pocket as the front piece from row 1 to row 10, note that the length of the foundation chain has changed. Leave a 1 m long yarn tail for sewing, cut yarn. Attach the bottom part of the tuck lock in the pocket, then place the pocket on top of the front piece right sides up. Sew the pocket in the front piece stitch by stitch between rows 10 and 11.

LID

Work 15 chain stitches to begin. Work the lid as the front piece from row 1 to row 11, note that the length of the foundation chain has changed. Work one more single stitch row, and for finishing, work one slip stitch row. Leave a 1 m (39 in) long yarn tail for sewing, cut yarn.

Attach the top part of the tuck lock in the middle front of the lid, then place the lid on top of the back piece right sides up. Sew the lid in place about 3 cm (1 ¼ in) from the top edge of the back piece. *Hey! The distance can be more or less than 3 cm (1 ¼ in) from the upper edge, this measure depends on your work.*

SEWING

Place the front piece and the back piece together right sides out, and crochet together with a slip stitch seam. Cut yarn and weave in ends.

Sew the short leather pieces on the backside of the work for the belt, and attach the belt in the work.

Veska

Chart

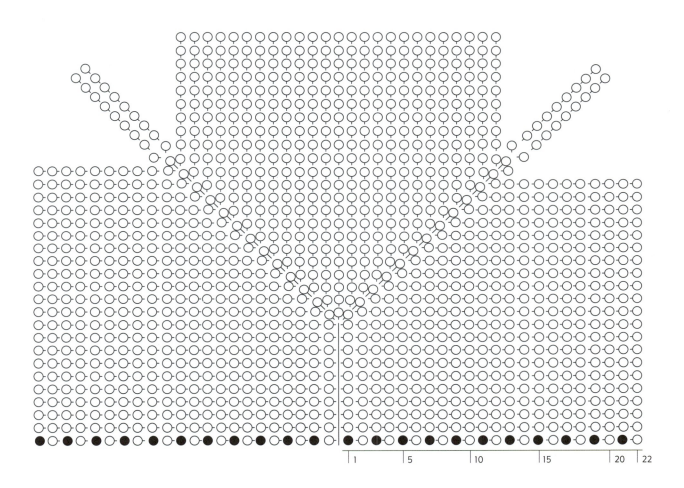

	foundation chain
○	single crochet stitch, sc
●	chain, ch

Construction

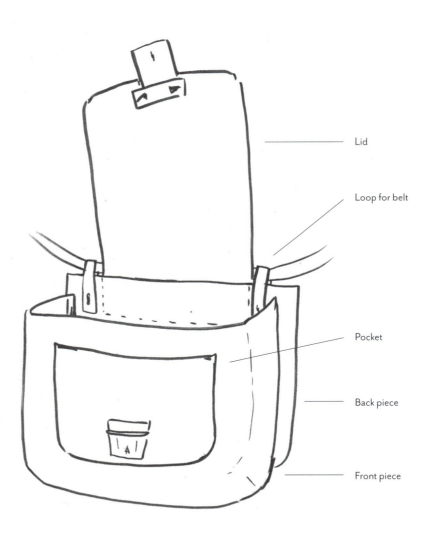

Lid

Loop for belt

Pocket

Back piece

Front piece

Aalto

When I was crocheting the Aalto rug, I imagined myself sitting by one of the fjords in the village of Sørvágur in the Faroe Islands at low tide. The water in the harbour disappears so quickly it leaves behind wavy sand ridges that the occasional seal will cross, leaving its mark. I had travelled to these islands in the Atlantic to teach crocheting, and once I saw from the airplane window the mythic islands rising from the sea, I was taken straight to another world.

One could marvel at the enchanting nature and the particular architecture of the turf roof houses, but it was those sand ridges at the bottom of the fjord that I drew in my sketchbook. Similar to those underwater shapes, the pattern in the Aalto rug is asymmetric.

Aalto rug

SIZE	w. 130 cm, l. 220 cm (w. 51 in, 87 in)
YARN	Frotee loopy craft yarn by Lankava
	(80% recycled cotton, 20% polyester,
	1.2 kg roll = 280 m / 2 lb 10 oz roll =
	306 yd), black 3 rolls, natural white 5 rolls
HOOK	9 mm (M / N-13)
GAUGE	7 sc x 7 row = 10 x 10 cm (4 x 4 in)

INFO

The rug is worked back and forth in single crochet stitches, carrying the other yarn inside the stitches throughout the work. Make sure not to pull the carry-on yarn too tight, keep it loose. Leave the carry-on yarn one stitch from the end of each row to make sure the yarn loops will not show on the right side of the work. Change the colour of the yarn in the last yarn over of the stitch.

ABBREVIATIONS

ch = chain stitch
st = stitch
sc = single crochet
yoh = yarn over hook
sl st = slip stitch

INSTRUCTIONS

Work 91 chain stitches in natural white yarn to begin, leave an 8 m (8 ¾ yd) long yarn tail for the slip stitch row.

ROW 1. Work 1 sc in the second st from the hook, grab the black yarn in the work. Work 1 sc in each st in natural white yarn leaving the black yarn one st from the end at the backside of the work. You have 90 sc on the row.

ROWS 2–4. Work 1 ch in natural white yarn, as this is the first sc of each row. Grab the black yarn in the work, work 1 sc in each st with natural white yarn.

ROW 5. Pattern begins. Work 1 ch in natural white yarn, grab the black yarn in the work. Work 4 sc, change to black yarn in the last yoh, work 5 sc in black yarn, change to natural white yarn in the last yoh, work 1 sc in each st until the end of row.

ROW 6. Work 1 ch in natural white yarn, grab the black yarn in the work. Work 43 sc in natural white yarn, change to black yarn in the last yoh. Work 8 sc in black yarn, 25 sc in natural white yarn, 10 sc in black yarn, and 3 sc in natural white yarn. *Hey! Since the next row starts in black yarn, change the colour of the yarn in the last yoh.*

ROWS 7–135. Follow the pattern chart. *Hey! Did you notice the waves of the pattern are non-symmetrical?* Pattern size of one black wave is 82 sc in width and 16 rows in height. Work the rows 132–135 in natural white yarn, carry the black yarn inside the sts.

Work a slip stitch row at both ends of the work in natural white yarn. Cut yarns and weave in ends.

Single crochet stitch, sc

Aalto

Chart

Potta

A busy farmer's market on the outskirts of Kutaisi; vendors packing their produce into coarse jute bags. We were in Georgia, sitting in a Chinese car with a trunk filled with khachapuri and honey we just bought from the market. In many other countries, our purchases would have instead been wrapped in plastic.

I always go for natural materials for my crochet projects. When you go through kilometre after kilometre of yarn, it makes sense to choose something that feels good between your fingers – cotton always trumps polyester. The coarse and beautiful material I have chosen for this basket reminds me of the dyed wool that I carried home from the Tusheti region of Georgia.

Potta basket

SIZE	h. 15 cm, d. 17 cm (h. 6 in, d. 6 ¾ in)
YARN	Filona linen cord, Lankava (100% linen, 500 g skein = 205 m / 1 lb 2 oz skein = 224 yd, Tex 1250/2), rosa 350 g (12 ½ oz)
HOOK	5 mm (H-8)
GAUGE	5 sc x 6 rows = 5 x 5 cm (2 x 2 in)
OTHER	2 metal rings d. 15 cm (6 in), 1 metal ring d. 3 cm (1 ¼ in)

INFO

The basket is made in a spiral in single crochet stitches starting from the bottom. Work a separate lid, reinforce the work by crocheting along a metal ring in the last rounds of the basket and the lid. Lastly, crochet a long shoulder strap for carrying the basket.

ABBREVIATIONS

rnd = round, rounds
ch = chain stitch
st = stitch
sc = single crochet stitch
sl st = slip stitch

INSTRUCTIONS

BASKET

RND 1. Roll yarn around a finger, work 8 sc in it. Work along the yarn tail, at the end of the round pull the yarn tail tight to close the hole.

RND 2. Work 2 sc in each st (16 sc). Continue to the second round in a spiral.

RND 3. Work 2 sc in every second st, 1 sc in other sts (24 sc).

RND 4. Work 2 sc in every third st, 1 sc in other sts (32 sc).

RND 5. Work 1 sc in each st.

RND 6. Work 2 sc in every fourth st, 1 sc in other sts (40 sc).

RND 7. Work 1 sc in each st.

RND 8. Work 2 sc in every fifth st, 1 sc in other sts (48 sc).

RNDS 9–22. Work 1 sc in each st.

RND 23. Grab the metal ring in the work, work 1 sc in each sts leaving the metal ring inside the sts.

RND 24. Work a reinforcing sc round on top of the sc sts from the previous round, work 1 elongated sc in each st. Cut yarn and weave in ends.

LID

Work a lid according to the basket pattern from round 1 to round 8.

RND 9. Grab a metal ring in the work, work 1 sc in the next 24 sts leaving the metal ring inside the sts, then work a loop of 16 ch sts (for buttons fastening), continue working

1 sc in the next 24 sts leaving the metal ring inside the sts. Leave a 1 m long yarn tail for sewing, cut yarn.

FINISHING

Work a 25 cm (10 in) long chain, weave it through the middle of the lid and tie a knot in both ends.

Sew the lid in place with a yarn tail with a few stitches making a yarn hinge. Make sure the lid holds steadily in place but also opens easily.

For the shoulder strap, work a 150 cm (59 in) long chain, weave it through the second last round of the basket and tie the ends in a tight knot.

Work a few sc sts around the small metal ring making it a button, sew the button in place in front of the basket.

Daisy

One of the entrants of a yarn-bombing competition had crocheted a big sunflower to the door handle of an office building. The person opening the door grabbed the flower stem and the big yellow flower bowed. I thought the idea was so hilarious, as office buildings are often as grey as the rainiest of days.

We had a similar goal when I took part in my friends' knit graffiti project in São Paulo. We talked and laughed for hours, and the table started to fill up with crocheted flowers designed to make people happy.

You can either decorate your home street with these daisies or attach them to your bag to carry around with you.

Daisy bag

SIZE	h. 28 cm, d. 24 cm (h. 11 in, d. 9 ½ in)
YARN	Liina and Molla twine, 12-ply, by Suomen Lanka (100% cotton, 500 g roll = 1280 m / 1 lb 2 oz roll = 1400 yd, Tex 30 x 12). For the bag: Liina, natural white 250 g (9 oz). For the daisies: Molla, yellow 100 g (3 ½ oz), white 200 g (7 oz).
HOOK	1.75 mm (US steel 6 / 7)
GAUGE	8 px x 8 rounds = 5 x 5 cm (2 x 2 in)
OTHER	leather base d. 12 cm (4 ¾ in) (28 holes punched around the base), cotton fabric for lining 40 x 70 cm (15 ¾ in x 27 ½ in), textile hardener, cotton rope for the handles 2.5 m (98 in)

INFO

The bag is made in pixel crochet technique around a leather base. The daisies are made separately and sewn into the bag. On the top edge of the bag, work openings for the handles. Before sewing in the flowers, brush a thin layer of textile hardener on the petals to prevent them from rolling.

ABBREVIATIONS

rnd = round, rounds
ch = chain stitch
st = stitch
sc = single crochet stitch
dc = double crochet stitch
sdc = starting double crochet stitch
yoh = yarn over hook
sl st = slip stitch

INSTRUCTIONS

BAG

Work the first round around the leather base with natural white yarn. Put the hook through the first of 28 holes, work 1 sc. Work *3 ch, 1 sc in the next hole*, repeat *–* until the end of the round. You have 112 sts in the work. Close round with a sl st.

RND 2. Work a sdc and 1 ch, work *1 dc, 1 ch* in each st. Close round with a sl st. You have 112 pixels on the round.

RNDS 3–43. Work a sdc and 1 ch, work *1 dc, 1 ch* in each st. Close round with a sl st.

RNDS 44–45. Top border. Work 2 sc in each pixel. You have 224 sts in the round.

RND 46. Openings for the handles. Work *5 sc, 5 ch, skip 5 sts, work 4 sc*, repeat *–* until the end of the round. You have 16 openings for the handles.

RNDS 47–48. Work 1 sc in each st. You have 224 sts in the round.

Work a slip stitch round. Cut yarn and weave in ends.

DAISY
SMALL STAMEN

RND 1. Roll a yarn loop around a finger with yellow yarn, close it with a sc, work 2 ch. Work 18 dc in the loop, carry the yarn tail inside the sts. Close round with a sl st. You now have 19 dc including the ch sts. To close the hole, pull the yarn tail tight.

RND 2. Work a sdc. Work *2 dc in the next st, 1 dc*, repeat *–* until the end of the round. You now have 28 dc in the work. Close round with a sl st. Cut yarn, and weave in ends.

Work 10 small stamens.

BIG STAMEN

Work rounds 1–2 as for the small stamen pattern.

RND 3. Work 1 ch, work 1 sc in each st. Leave a 1 m (39 in) long yarn tail for sewing, cut yarn. *Hey! You may have noticed that the bigger stamen is a bit plump. Good!*

Work 10 big stamen.

PETALS

Work 14 petals around each small stamen with white yarn. Work 1 sc in the last st of a stamen. Work 14 ch, turn, work 1 dc in the fourth st from the hook. Work 1 dc in the next 10 sts. Close the first petal with a sc in the next st of the stamen. Work 1 sc, 14 ch, turn, work 1 dc in the fourth st from the hook, 1 dc in the next 10 sts, close the second petal with a sc in the stamen. Continue working the petals with the same pattern, working altogether 14 petals. Close round with a sl st.

Work a slip stitch round around the petals. Work 1 sl st in each st, and 1 sl st between sc sts (at the base of the petals). Cut yarn and weave in ends.

Join small and big stamens together with a slip stitch seam. Place the bigger stamen on top of the small stamen right sides out, put the hook through both layers, and work 1 sl st in each st to join the stamens together. Cut yarn and weave in ends.

Work all 10 daisies with the same pattern.

Hey! If the flower petals are rolling inwards, apply a thin layer of textile hardener on the backside of the petals, and leave to dry.

Sew the flowers in the bag.

Daisy Chart, bag

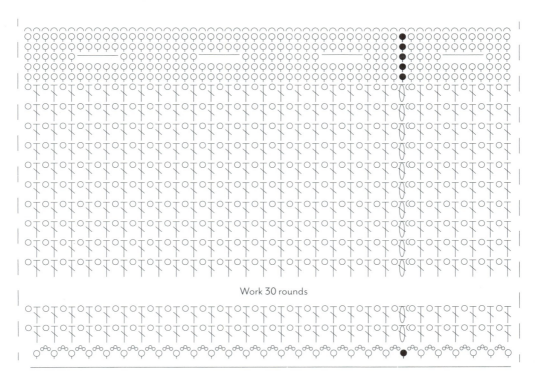

Work 30 rounds

Leather base

○	chain, ch
⫚	starting double crochet stitch, sdc
⊤	double crochet stitch, dc
⊂	slip stitch, sl st
♀	single crochet stitch, sc
●	first sc of the round
——	opening for a handle, work 5 ch

Daisy

Chart, daisy

Small stamen,
petals

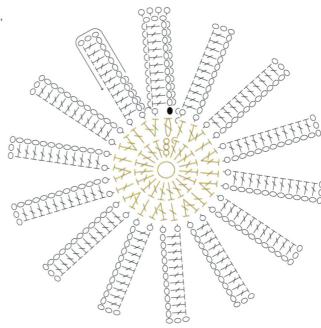

Big stamen

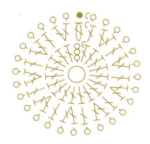

⭕	starting loop
◦ ⚪	chain, ch
⸶	starting double crochet stitch, sdc
⊤ ⊤	double crochet stitch, dc
⋎	increase, 2 dc worked in a same st
((	slip stitch, sl st
⚲ ⚲	single crochet stitch, sc
● ●	first st of the round

LINING

Cut a lining according to the size of your bag. Sew the lining inside the bag between rows 1 and 44 by hand.

Weave the cotton rope handle through the openings on top of the bag.

Vuokko

The Vuokko pattern is like a beautiful band of plumeria flowers. The plumeria plant, the flowers of which contain healing natural remedies, comes from Central America. On one of my trips, I was told that by placing a plumeria flower behind your right ear, you are signalling a desire for company. What a great alternative to a dating app!

See how the Vuokko pattern looks when worked with three colours, by crocheting the round centre of the flower with a yellow yarn. Use the pattern to crochet the adorable wallet as well as the beautiful beach rug for your summer holiday.

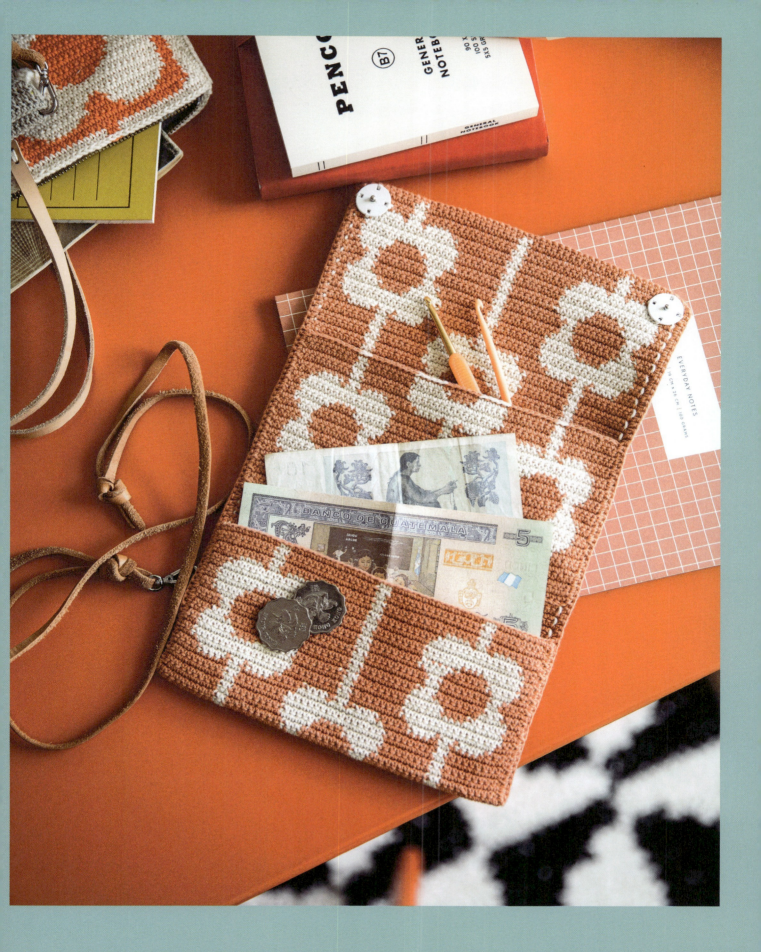

Vuokko wallet

SIZE	w. 18 cm, l. 38 cm (full length) (w. 7 in, l. 15 in)
YARN	Liina cotton twine, 12-ply, by Suomen Lanka (100% cotton, 500 g roll = 1280 m / 1 lb 2 oz roll = 1400 yd, Tex 30 x 12), natural white 50 g (1 ¾ oz), Molla cotton twine, 12-ply, by Suomen Lanka, brown 100 g (3 ½ oz)
HOOK	1.75 mm (US steel 6 / 7)
GAUGE	16 sc x 15 rows = 5 x 5 cm (2 x 2 in)
OTHER	thin leather strap 1 m (39 in), small snap hook, small D-ring, 2 snap buttons

INFO

The wallet is worked back and forth in single crochet stitches, carrying the other yarn inside the stitches throughout the work. Make sure not to pull the carry-on yarn too tight, keep it loose. Leave the carry-on yarn one stitch from the end of each row to make sure the yarn loops will not show on the right side of the work. Change the colour of the yarn in the last yarn over of the stitch.

ABBREVIATIONS

ch = chain stitch
st = stitch
sc = single crochet
yoh = yarn over hook
sl st = slip stitch

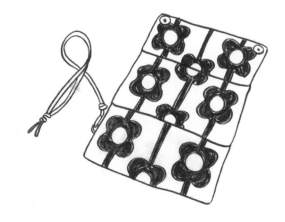

INSTRUCTIONS

Work 57 chain stitches in brown yarn to begin.

ROW 1. Work 1 sc in the second st from the hook, grab the natural white yarn in the work. *Hey! Work this row in the back loops of the chain stitches.* Work 9 sc, change to natural white yarn in the last yoh. Work 2 sc in natural white yarn, 15 sc in brown yarn, 2 sc in natural white yarn, 15 sc in brown yarn, 2 sc in natural white yarn, 10 sc in brown yarn. Leave the natural white yarn one st from the end at the backside of the work. You now have 56 sc in the work.

ROWS 2–4. Work 1 ch in brown yarn, as this is the first sc of each row. Grab the natural white yarn in the work and work as for row 1.

ROW 5. Work 1 ch in brown yarn, work 4 sc, change to natural white yarn. Work 4 sc in natural white yarn, 1 sc in brown yarn, 2 sc in natural white yarn, 1 sc in brown yarn, 4 sc in natural white yarn, 10 sc in brown yarn, 2 sc in natural white yarn, 10 sc in brown yarn, 4 sc in natural white yarn, 1 sc in brown yarn, 2 sc in natural white yarn, 1 sc in brown yarn, 4 sc natural white yarn and 5 sc in brown yarn.

ROWS 6–113. Follow the pattern chart. Work altogether 113 rows. Cut yarns and weave in ends.

POCKETS

Pocket 2 is made according to the pattern chart. Work rows 60 to 86 as for the wallet. The width of the pocket is 56 sts, the height of the pocket is 26 rows. Work a slip stitch row on the top edge of the pocket. Cut yarns, weave in ends.

Place the work on a table wrong side up. Place pocket 2 between rows 60 and 68 right side up, sew the bottom edge into the wallet. The sides of the pocket will be closed later.

Fold the lower part of the wallet inwards from row 27, as this forms a second pocket (pocket 1) that is 26 rows in height. Pin the pocket in place. The sides of the pocket will be closed later.

BORDER

Crochet a border on the three sides of the wallet with single crochet stitches with brown yarn. In this round, close the sides of both pockets.

To make the border, place the work on a table right side up, starting from the right bottom corner. Put the hook through both layers of the work, work 13 sc. Place the small D-ring in the work, leaving it inside the next 4 sc sts. Continue working the border, work 1 sc in each row. In the two top corners, work 3 sc in the same st. Cut yarn and weave in ends.

Fold the work in shape, pockets inside, and a lid on top. Measure a place for two snap buttons to close the lid, sew in place by hand.

Tie the leather strap in the snap hook and attach the handle in place.

☐ ■ Single crochet stitch, sc

Vuokko

Chart

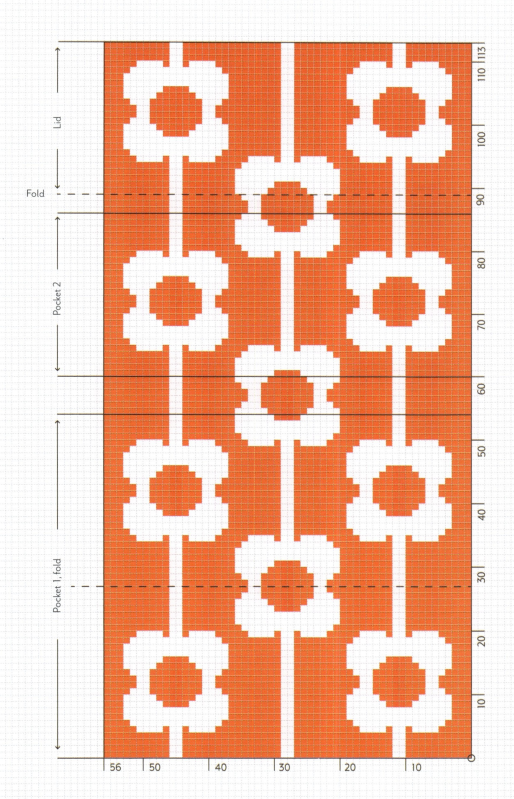

Vuokko pattern, detail from a symbol chart.   ○ ● Single crochet stitch, sc

VUOKKO BEACH RUG Work the beach rug
as for Vuokko wallet. The size of the rug is
56 sc in width and 174 rows in height.

SIZE w. 45 cm, l. 150 cm (w. 18 in, l. 59 in)
YARN Moi yarn by Molla Mills for Lankava (80% recycled
cotton, 20% polyester), black 500 g (1 lb 2 oz), natural
white 1 kg (2 lb 3 oz)
HOOK 5 mm (H-8)
GAUGE 13 sc x 13 rows = 10 cm x 10 cm (4 x 4 in)

Handcrafts – Connecting People

I was waiting for a bullet train at a station in Chiyoda, Tokyo, with my crocheted bag, at the bottom of which was an onigiri, crushed by my camera. In a few hours, I would hold a crochet workshop in a handcraft store in Osaka, and I had that fluttery feeling of butterflies, chō in Japanese, in my stomach. At Narita airport I had rented an overpriced pocket wi-fi and was now able to open the map application, check my whereabouts and send the coordinates home.

I really was in Japan. Never had I travelled this far from Finland. I had been brought to Japan by the same passion that a year earlier had led me to India to discover wonderful scents and to explore the mountainous tea-producing regions.

In Japan, I taught several crochet workshops where the makers sat in silent concentration, and I heard only the low voice of the interpreter – it was a beautifully serene atmosphere. I always travelled to the teaching location via bullet train, gazing out of the window; but for the first snow, which had already fallen in Shizuoka, I would have been able to see the peak of Mount Fuji.

The workshops I held in the heat of Brazil, however, were the complete opposite of this Japanese harmony. The classrooms were filled with loud, excited talk and tens of pairs of hands were already eagerly crocheting flowers while I was still in the middle of my welcome speech.

Even though countries and cultures vary, we makers always have one thing in common: a sense of community. When I pack my bags in the north and travel to another continent to teach crochet, it always feels as though I am travelling to meet old friends.

Sharing my own passion with others has taught me something important. It does not really matter where you are, it is the people around you that bring everything to life. So turn your crocheting into a communal effort, get to know your fellow makers and share your knowledge and skills.

One day you might end up driving through Europe in a Renault, alongside a crocheter you met at a workshop, making precious moments together!

♥ Molla

Yarn Information

Alpaca Brush by Bettaknit.
44% alpaca, 44% wool, 12% polyamide,
50 g roll = 200 m (1 ¾ oz roll = 218 yd).

Filona jute cord, Lankava. 100% jute,
500 g roll = 225 m (1 lb 2 oz roll =
246 yd), Tex 280 x 8.

Filona linen cord, Lankava. 100% linen,
500 g skein = 205 m (1 lb 2 oz skein =
224 yd), Tex 1250/2.

Filona flat paper ribbon, Lankava.
100% paper, 100 g skein = 87 m (3 ½ oz
skein = 95 yd), 0,80 Nm, Tex 1250.

Frotee loopy craft yarn by Lankava.
80% recycled cotton, 20% polyester,
1.2 kg roll = 280 m (2 lb 10 oz roll = 306 yd).

Highland Yarn by Kit Couture.
100 % wool, 50 g roll = 100 m (1 ¾ oz
roll = 109 yd).

**Liina twine (12-ply) by Suomen
Lanka.** 100% cotton, 500 g roll =1280 m
(1 lb 2 oz roll = 1400 yd), Tex 30 x 12.

**Liina twine (18-ply) by Suomen
Lanka.** 100% cotton, 500 g roll = 840 m
(1 lb 2 oz roll = 918 yd), Tex 30 x 18.

Matilda yarn by Lankava. 80% recycled
cotton, 20% polyester, 500 g roll = 140 m
(1 lb 2 oz roll =153 yd).

Mini tube yarn by Lankava.
80% recycled cotton, 20% polyester,
1 kg roll = 335 m (2 lb 3 oz roll = 366 yd).

Moi yarn by Molla Mills for Lankava.
80% recycled cotton, 20% polyester,
200 g roll (7 oz).

**Molla twine (12-ply) by Suomen
Lanka.** 100% cotton, 500 g roll = 1280 m
(1 lb 2 oz roll =1400 yd), Tex 30 x 12.

**Molla twine (18-ply) by Suomen
Lanka.** 100% cotton, 500 g roll = 840 m
(1 lb 2 oz roll = 918 yd), Tex 30 x 18.

**Moppari twisted mop yarn by Suomen
Lanka.** 80% recycled cotton,
20% polyester, 1 kg roll = 310 m (2 lb 3 oz
roll = 339 yd), Tex 100 x 10 x 3.

Muhku wool by Lankava.
100% wool, 1 kg roll = 390 m (2 lb 3 oz
roll = 426 yd), Tex 850 x 3.

Prato Cotton by Bettaknit.
100% recycled cotton, 100 g roll =
100 m (3 ½ oz roll = 109 yd).

Varppi twine by Suomen Lanka.
100% cotton, 500 g roll = 500 m
(1 lb 2 oz roll = 546 yd), Tex 50 x 18.

This edition published in 2022 by Hardie Grant Books, an imprint of Hardie Grant Publishing
First published in 2021 by Laine Publishing Oy
Published in agreement with Ferly Agency

Hardie Grant Books (Melbourne)
Wurundjeri Country
Building 1, 658 Church Street
Richmond, Victoria 3121

Hardie Grant Books (London)
5th & 6th Floors
52–54 Southwark Street
London SE1 1UN

hardiegrantbooks.com

A catalogue record for this book is available from the National Library of Australia

Crochet Crush
ISBN 978 1 74379 898 0

10 9 8 7 6 5 4 3 2

PHOTOGRAPHS: Emma Sarpaniemi, Jonna Hietala & Sini Kramer
LAYOUT: Irina Kauppinen
STYLIST: Anna Komonen
HMUA: Miika Kemppainen
MODELS: Landys & Monica / As You Are Agency
CLOTHES & PROPS: Havaianas, Iittala, Kokori, New Balance, Terhi Pölkki, Vimma, Vuokko, & Other Stories

The making of this book has been supported by Suomen Tietokirjailijat ry.

Colour reproduction by Splitting Image Colour Studio
Printed in China by Leo Paper Products LTD.

The paper this book is printed on is from FSC®-certified forests and other sources. FSC® promotes environmentally responsible, socially beneficial and economically viable management of the world's forests.